LOVE IN THE LUXURY LANE

BY

PAMMIE LOVE

COPYRIGHT © 2024 PAMMIE LOVE

All rights reserved. No part of this publication may be reproduced, distributed, or transmitted in any form or by any means, including photocopying, recording, or other electronic or mechanical methods, without the prior written permission of the publisher, except in the case of brief quotations embodied in critical reviews and certain other noncommercial uses permitted by copyright law.

DEDICATION

To those who dream without limits and love without boundaries, this story is yours.

To my family, the unshakable pillars of my life—your love, encouragement, and faith in me have been the guiding light that made this journey possible. You are the heart of everything I do.

To the readers who seek a world where luxury meets love, and where every page offers a new adventure—thank you for choosing to immerse yourselves in this story. Your trust in my words means more than you know.

And to every soul that believes in the magic of a love story as grand and eternal as the stars themselves, may these pages bring you the romance, passion, and wonder that your heart desires.

This novel is dedicated to you, with all my heart.

ACKNOWLEDGMENTS

I would like to extend my deepest gratitude to the incredible individuals who brought this novel to life.

To my cherished loved ones, your unwavering support and boundless patience have been my guiding light. Thank you for believing in me even when I doubted myself.

To my editor and beta readers, your keen insights and thoughtful feedback were invaluable in shaping this story. Your dedication and attention to detail have truly elevated "Love in the Luxury Lane."

To the authors whose billionaire romance novels have inspired me, thank you for blazing the trail and showing that love, in all its opulence and complexity, can indeed conquer all.

And to you, my dear readers, thank you for choosing to immerse yourself in the world of "Love in the Luxury Lane." I hope these pages bring you joy, passion, and just the right touch of luxury. Your support and enthusiasm mean the world to me, and I can't wait to share more stories with you in the future.

Thank you, from the bottom of my heart, for being part of this journey.

TABLE OF CONTENTS

DEDICATION ii
ACKNOWLEDGMENTS iii
PREFACE viii
CHAPTER ONE 1
MIDNIGHT ENCOUNTER 1
CHAPTER TWO 12
WHISPERS IN THE DARK 12
CHAPTER THREE 23
SHADOWS OF THE PAST 23
CHAPTER FOUR 31
THE INTERVIEW 31
CHAPTER FIVE 42
THE MYSTERIOUS MR. BLACKWOOD 42
CHAPTER SIX 52
THE UNEXPECTED ENCOUNTER 52
CHAPTER SEVEN 61
THE PROPOSITION 61
CHAPTER EIGHT 69
THE STALKER 69
CHAPTER NINE 77
CROSSING BOUNDARIES 77
CHAPTER TEN 88
SECRETS AND LIES 88

CHAPTER ELEVEN	99
THE SHADOWS CLOSE IN	99
CHAPTER TWELVE	106
THE MASK SLIPS	106
CHAPTER THIRTEEN	111
BENEATH THE SURFACE	111
CHAPTER FOURTEEN	117
INTO THE ABYSS	117
CHAPTER FIFTEEN	128
THE FALLOUT	128
CHAPTER SIXTEEN	138
THE RECKONING	138
CHAPTER SEVENTEEN	163
NEW BEGINNINGS	163
CHAPTER EIGHTEEN	173
UNFINISHED BUSINESS	173
CHAPTER NINETEEN	188
THE FINAL CONFRONTATION	188
CHAPTER TWENTY	204
BREAKING FREE	204
CHAPTER TWENTY-ONE	216
REDEMPTION	216
CHAPTER TWENTY-TWO	226
LOVE IN THE LUXURY LANE	226
CHAPTER TWENTY-THREE	238

THE TRUTH REVEALED 238
CHAPTER TWENTY-FOUR 250
FOREVER FREE 250
EPILOGUE 264
HAPPILY EVER AFTER 264

PREFACE

"Ah, love. That elusive, intoxicating feeling can sweep us off our feet and leave us breathless. I've always been fascinated by how it can transform us, making us feel seen, heard, and understood in a way that nothing else can. Like a warm embrace on a cold day, love has the power to comfort and heal us, to make us feel whole.

As I sit here with you, sipping my coffee and sharing this story, I'm reminded of the countless times I've witnessed love's power—the way it can bring people together, create new beginnings, and heal old wounds. I think of the couples who've found each other despite the odds, who've fought for their love and made it last. I think of the families who've been torn apart by conflict, only to find their way back to each other through the power of forgiveness and love.

But what happens when love becomes an obsession? When the lines between passion and possession blur, and the very thing that once brought us joy becomes a source of pain? When the desire to love and be loved turns into a need to control and possess?

That's when love can become toxic, suffocating, and even dangerous.

Meet Lexi, a bright and beautiful young woman with a heart full of hope and a past that's left her wary of love. She's been hurt before, and the scars still linger. But she's also fiercely independent, determined to make a life for herself on her terms. And then there's Beckett, a wealthy and charismatic billionaire with a reputation for getting what he wants, no matter the cost. He's used to being in control, to calling the shots and getting his way.

Their story is one of love, lust, and the blurred lines between the two. It's a tale of obsession, control, and the fight for freedom. It's a reminder that, no matter how dark things may seem, love can always be redeemed. But it's also a warning: that the price of love can sometimes be too high to pay.

As we journey into the world of Love in the Luxury Lane, I invite you to reflect on your own experiences with love. Have you ever felt the rush of falling for someone, only to realize that it wasn't meant to be?

Have you ever loved someone so much that you lost yourself in the process? Have you ever had to fight for your independence, for the right to love and be loved on your terms?

These are the questions that Lexi and Beckett will face, and the answers they find will change them forever. So, dear reader, grab a cup of your favorite brew, get comfortable, and join me on this journey into the heart of love. Let's explore the highs and lows together, and discover that, in the end, true freedom can only be found in the heart."

CHAPTER ONE

MIDNIGHT ENCOUNTER

A talented event planner is working late at the luxurious Bellevue Manor in Manhattan. Lexi Thompson, 28, hair in a messy bun, glasses slightly askew. She's hunched over a desk, surrounded by a sea of papers, fabric swatches, and empty coffee cups. The room? It's bigger than her entire apartment.

Imagine a space so grand it makes your jaw drop. That's the Bellevue Manor ballroom. Think marble floors, crystal chandeliers, and walls that could tell stories of a thousand elegant affairs. It's like stepping into a different world, one where luxury isn't just a word, it's a way of life.

And there, amid all this splendor, is Lexi Thompson. She's a vision of organized chaos, buried under stacks of papers, a rainbow of fabric swatches, and more coffee cups than she can count. Her hair, usually a sleek brunette curtain, is now a messy bun, with stray strands sticking out rebelliously. Her glasses, slightly askew, give her an endearingly frazzled look. Despite

the exhaustion etched on her face, her eyes are sharp and focused. She's in her element.

Lexi loves her job, but on nights like these, when the world outside is quiet and she's alone with her thoughts, she wonders if it's worth it. The glamorous events, the high-profile clients, the perfection she strives for—it's all-consuming. But she's good at it. Good. And in the cutthroat world of Manhattan event planning, being good isn't enough. You have to be the best.

She glanced at the clock. Midnight. Typical. The silence of the manor was both a comfort and a reminder of her solitude. She sighed, rubbing her temples. Just a few more touches and the ballroom will be ready for tomorrow's event. The thought of sleep was a distant dream.

A faint sound pulled her from her reverie. She straightened, ears straining. There it was again—a soft shuffle, barely audible. Her heart rate picked up, and a twinge of anxiety crept in. Bellevue Manor was supposed to be empty, except for her. She stood the creak of her chair unnervingly loud in the stillness.

"Hello?" Her voice echoed, bouncing off the grand walls. She waited, holding her breath. Nothing. She shook her head, chastising herself. "Get a grip, Lexi. You're just tired."

Determined to finish, she bent over her work again, but the uneasy feeling lingered. It was like being watched, a prickling sensation at the back of her neck. She shook it off, focusing on the centerpiece arrangements. Each flower had to be perfect, every detail in its place.

Another noise, this time closer. Her head snapped up, eyes wide. The dim lighting cast long shadows, turning the opulent room into a scene from a gothic novel. She squinted, trying to pierce the darkness at the far end of the ballroom.

There, among the shadows, stood a figure. Tall, imposing, and unmistakably masked. Lexi's breath caught in her throat. The room seemed to shrink, the air thick with tension. She opened her mouth to speak, but no sound came out. Panic surged, and she took a step back, her heel catching on the edge of a rug.

The masked figure remained still, an eerie statue. Lexi's mind raced. Who could it be? Why were they here? Every horror movie she'd ever seen flashed through her mind. She needed to get out, now.

Summoning her courage, she turned and bolted towards the door, her heels clicking frantically on the marble floor. She reached the grand doors, fingers fumbling with the handle. Just as she threw them open, she risked a glance back. The figure was gone. Vanished as if it had never been there.

She stumbled into the hallway, breath coming in ragged gasps. The cool air hit her face, a stark contrast to the heat of her fear. She didn't stop running until she was outside, the towering manor behind her, its dark windows like watching eyes.

Fumbling with her phone, she dialed security, her hands shaking. As she waited for the call to connect, she glanced back at the manor, its grand silhouette imposing against the night sky. What had she just witnessed? Who was that masked figure? Questions swirled in her mind, but one thing was clear—something was very wrong at Bellevue Manor.

Lexi sat on the curb, the cool concrete grounding her. The security guards arrived, their flashlights cutting through the darkness as they searched the manor. She

wrapped her arms around herself, trying to calm the storm of thoughts in her head.

"You okay, miss?" one of the guards asked, his voice gentle but wary.

Lexi nodded, though she didn't feel okay. "I saw someone inside. A masked figure. I don't know who it was, but it didn't feel right."

The guard exchanged a look with his partner. "We'll check it out. Stay here."

As they moved into the manor, Lexi's mind drifted. Who could it have been? A prank? An intruder? The possibilities were endless, each one more unsettling than the last. She shivered, not from the cold, but from the lingering fear. She had always felt safe in Bellevue Manor, its grandeur a comforting presence. Now, it felt like a labyrinth of shadows and secrets.

Minutes stretched into what felt like hours before the guards returned. "We didn't find anyone," the first guard said, shaking his head. "No signs of forced entry, nothing out of place."

Lexi frowned. "But I saw them. I know I did."

"I believe you," he replied, his tone kind but skeptical. "Maybe you should take the night off, and get some rest. We'll keep an eye on the place."

She wanted to argue, to insist that she wasn't crazy, but the exhaustion was overwhelming. Nodding, she stood, her legs feeling unsteady. "Yeah, maybe you're right. Thanks."

As she walked away, the weight of the night pressing down on her, Lexi couldn't shake the feeling that this was just the beginning. Something had changed, and she had a nagging suspicion that her life was about to get a lot more complicated.

Back at her small Brooklyn Heights apartment, Lexi collapsed onto her couch, the events of the night replaying in her mind. She stared at the ceiling, the darkness of her room a stark contrast to the bright,

opulent manor. The masked figure haunted her thoughts, a shadow she couldn't escape.

She reached for her phone, hesitating before dialing. "Hey, it's me," she said when the familiar voice answered. "Can we talk? I need to clear my head."

Within minutes, her best friend, Emma, was at her door, a comforting presence. "What happened?" Emma asked, concern etched on her face.

Lexi recounted the night's events, the fear, the masked figure, the search. Emma listened, nodding sympathetically. "That sounds terrifying. Are you sure it wasn't just a trick of the light? You've been under a lot of stress."

Lexi shook her head. "I know what I saw, Emma. It was real."

Emma sighed, pulling Lexi into a hug. "We'll figure it out. Maybe it's time to take a break and get some rest. You've been pushing yourself too hard."

As comforting as Emma's words were, Lexi couldn't shake the feeling that something more was at play. She nodded, though, knowing her friend was right. Rest was what she needed, even if her mind refused to quiet down.

As the night wore on, Lexi finally drifted into a fitful sleep, dreams plagued by masked figures and shadowy corners. She awoke the next morning with a start, the memory of the previous night still fresh in her mind.

Determined not to let fear control her, Lexi got ready for the day, her resolve hardening. She would go back to Bellevue Manor, finish her work, and prove to herself that she could handle whatever came her way. The world of luxury and high stakes didn't leave room for fear.

But as she stepped into the grand ballroom once again, a chill ran down her spine. The room was exactly as she'd left it, yet it felt different. Haunted, almost. She took a deep breath, shaking off the unease. Today was a new day, and she had a job to do.

Lexi threw herself into her work, her hands moving with practiced precision as she adjusted centerpieces, checked lighting, and ensured every detail was perfect. The event tonight was crucial, and she couldn't afford any mistakes.

As the day wore on, the manor came to life with the buzz of activity. Her team arrived, and the final preparations began. The earlier incident faded into the background, replaced by the whirlwind of tasks and last-minute changes.

But as the evening approached and guests began to arrive, Lexi couldn't shake the feeling that she was

being watched. She glanced around, her eyes scanning the crowd for any sign of the masked figure. Nothing. Just the usual array of well-dressed socialites and businessmen, mingling under the chandeliers.

Taking a moment to catch her breath, she stepped out onto the balcony, the cool evening air a welcome relief. She leaned against the railing, her mind racing. Who could that figure have been? And why were they there?

Her thoughts were interrupted by a voice behind her. "Everything okay?"

She turned to see one of the caterers, a kind-faced young man named Ben. She offered a small smile. "Yeah, just needed a breather. It's been a long day."

Ben nodded sympathy in his eyes. "I hear you. These events can be crazy. But you've got this. You always do."

Lexi appreciated the reassurance. "Thanks, Ben. That means a lot."

As Ben returned to his duties, Lexi stayed on the balcony, letting the city's sounds wash over her. She couldn't let fear control her. Whoever that figure was, they wouldn't scare her away from the job she loved.

With renewed determination, she headed back inside, ready to face whatever came her way. The night was still young, and she had a feeling it would be one to remember.

The event was a success, the guests mingling and laughing, the atmosphere buzzing with excitement. Lexi moved through the crowd, her professional smile in place, making sure everything ran smoothly.

But even as she engaged in polite conversation, her mind kept drifting back to the masked figure.

It wasn't until the end of the night, as the last guests were leaving and the manor was quieting down, that she allowed herself to relax. She wandered through the now-empty ballroom, the remnants of the evening's festivities scattered around.

A soft sound made her freeze. She turned slowly, her heart pounding. There, standing at the edge of the room, was the masked figure. Just as imposing, just as silent.

Lexi's breath caught. She took a step forward, then another. "Who are you?" she demanded, her voice trembling despite her attempt at bravery. "Why are you here?"

The figure didn't move, didn't speak. It was as if they were waiting for something. Lexi felt a surge of frustration and fear. She took another step, her hand reaching out as if to pull the mask away.

But before she could touch them, the figure turned and vanished into the shadows, disappearing through a side door. Lexi stood there, her hand still outstretched, her mind reeling. What was happening? Who was this person?

She knew she couldn't let this go. She had to find out the truth, no matter what it took. As she stood in the empty ballroom, the weight of the night pressing down on her, Lexi made a silent vow. She would uncover the mystery of the masked figure, and she wouldn't stop until she did.

The night was far from over. And so was Lexi's journey into the unknown.

CHAPTER TWO

WHISPERS IN THE DARK

Lexi Thompson, back at her apartment in Brooklyn Heights, thought she had left the eerie events of Bellevue Manor behind her. She craved the familiarity of her cozy, eclectic home, a sanctuary amidst the chaos of her demanding career. Yet, tonight, her sanctuary felt anything but safe.

Let me paint a picture for you. Lexi's apartment isn't what you'd expect for a high-flying Manhattan event planner. It's small but charming, filled with personal touches that reflect her personality. Think mismatched furniture, artfully cluttered bookshelves, and a faint scent of lavender in the air. It's a place that screams Lexi—warm, welcoming, and utterly unique.

Tonight, though, something felt off. The air was thick with unease, an intangible weight pressing down on her. She shook her head, trying to dismiss the feeling. It's just the aftermath of a long day, she told herself. But the memory of the masked figure at Bellevue Manor lingered, a shadow she couldn't escape.

She kicked off her heels, sinking into her worn leather couch with a sigh. The silence of her apartment, usually a comfort, felt oppressive. She picked up her phone, scrolling mindlessly through messages, hoping for a distraction.

A soft creak made her freeze. Her heart skipped a beat, and her mind immediately jumped to the worst conclusion. But *it's just the old wood floors*, she reasoned. *This building has been around forever.*

Still, she couldn't shake the feeling of being watched. She glanced around, eyes darting to the corners of the room, half-expecting to see the masked figure lurking there. Nothing. Just shadows and silence.

"Get a grip, Lexi," she muttered to herself, rubbing her temples. "You're being paranoid."

She stood, deciding that a hot shower might help. The bathroom was her favorite part of the apartment, a little oasis with its claw foot tub and vintage tiles. The water cascaded over her, washing away the day's stress. She closed her eyes, letting the steam envelop her.

But even here, in her safe space, she couldn't escape the feeling. It was as if the shadows themselves were whispering to her, a sinister presence just out of sight. She shivered, despite the heat.

After her shower, she wrapped herself in a plush robe, trying to shake off the lingering unease. She made her way to the kitchen, deciding a cup of chamomile tea might help. As she waited for the water to boil, her eyes kept straying to the window. The city lights flickered outside, but tonight they felt more like watchful eyes than comforting beacons.

The kettle whistled, startling her. She poured the hot water over the tea bag, watching the steam curl into the air. Taking a deep breath, she tried to calm her racing heart. It's just your imagination, she repeated.

Sitting at the small kitchen table, she sipped her tea, the warmth soothing her frayed nerves. She needed to distract herself, to get her mind off the figure and the unsettling feeling that had followed her home.

Reaching for her laptop, she decided to do some work. There was always something to plan, an event to coordinate, details to perfect. As she immersed herself in the familiar rhythm of schedules and spreadsheets, the tension began to ease.

But then, a soft thud echoed through the apartment. Her head snapped up, eyes wide. She set the laptop aside, standing slowly. "Hello?" Her voice sounded small, even to her ears.

Silence. She took a cautious step toward the hallway, heart pounding in her chest. Another thud, this time closer. Her breath quickened. She grabbed a candlestick from the table—an improvised weapon, but it gave her a small sense of security.

As she moved through the apartment, every creak of the floorboards seemed amplified, every shadow more menacing. She reached the bedroom, the source of the noise. The door was ajar, a sliver of darkness spilling into the hall.

Pushing the door open with the candlestick, she peered inside. Nothing seemed out of place. She let out a breath she hadn't realized she was holding. But then she saw it—a piece of paper, fluttering on her bed.

Cautiously, she approached, picking up the note. Her blood ran cold as she read the words scrawled in neat, precise handwriting: "You can't escape me."

Her heart raced, a mix of fear and anger surging through her. Who was doing this? And why? She scanned the room, looking for any sign of the intruder. But the apartment was silent, empty except for her.

Clutching the note, she backed out of the room, her mind racing. She needed help and needed to tell someone. Emma. She dialed her friend's number, her hands trembling.

"Lexi? What's wrong?" Emma's voice was filled with concern.

"Someone's been in my apartment," Lexi said, her voice shaking. "I found a note. They're watching me, Emma."

"Oh my God. Are you safe? Do you want me to come over?"

Lexi glanced around, feeling the weight of the shadows. "No, I think I need to get out of here. Can I come to your place?"

"Of course. Come over right now. I'll be waiting."

She hung up, grabbing her keys and a few essentials. As she stepped into the hallway, she couldn't shake the feeling of eyes on her back. She hurried to her car, the city's usual hustle and bustle feeling distant and surreal.

The drive to Emma's felt like a blur. Her mind was a whirlwind of fear and questions. Who was this masked figure? Why were they targeting her? And how had they found her here?

Emma's apartment was a haven of warmth and light, a stark contrast to the oppressive darkness of Lexi's place. Emma pulled her into a tight hug as soon as she walked through the door. "You're safe now," she murmured.

Lexi clung to her friend, the tears she'd been holding back finally spilling over. "I'm so scared, Emma. I don't know who this person is or what they want."

Emma guided her to the couch, sitting beside her. "We'll figure it out. First, we need to call the police. They need to know what's going on."

Lexi nodded, grateful for Emma's level-headedness. They made the call, and soon two officers were at the apartment, taking her statement. Lexi described the events at Bellevue Manor, the masked figure, and the note in her apartment. The officers listened intently, their expressions serious.

"We'll increase patrols in your area," one of them said. "And we'll look into any recent reports of similar incidents. In the meantime, it's a good idea to stay with a friend."

Lexi thanked them, feeling a little safer but still shaken. After the officers left, Emma made them both a cup of tea, her presence a comforting balm to Lexi's frayed nerves.

"Why do you think this person is targeting you?" Emma asked, her brow furrowed with concern.

"I have no idea," Lexi admitted. "It all started at Bellevue Manor. I saw the figure there, and now this. It doesn't make any sense."

Emma squeezed her hand. "We'll figure it out. You're not alone in this, Lexi."

Lexi nodded, feeling a surge of gratitude for her friend's unwavering support. They spent the rest of the evening talking, Emma's steady presence a comforting anchor in the storm of Lexi's fear.

But even as they chatted about mundane things—work, plans for the weekend, a new restaurant Emma wanted to try—Lexi couldn't shake the feeling of being watched. Every creak of the apartment, every shadow in the corner of her eye, set her on edge.

She tried to push the fear aside, to focus on the warmth of Emma's friendship and the safety of her surroundings. But as the night wore on and the city outside grew quiet, the unease settled deep in her bones.

That night, Lexi lay in Emma's guest room, staring at the ceiling. Sleep felt impossible, her mind a whirl of anxiety and questions. She kept replaying the events of the past few days, trying to make sense of them. Who was the masked figure? Why were they stalking her? And what did they want?

She sighed, turning over and hugging her pillow. The guest room was cozy, decorated in Emma's eclectic style, with bright colors and soft textures. It should have been comforting, but tonight it felt like a stranger's room, unfamiliar and unsettling.

She closed her eyes, willing herself to sleep. But every time she drifted off, she was jolted awake by the phantom sound of footsteps, the memory of the note's chilling message.

"You can't escape me."

The words echoed in her mind, a sinister promise that kept her on edge. She glanced at the clock. 3:00 a.m.

She groaned, sitting up and running a hand through her hair. She needed to do something, anything, to calm her racing thoughts.

Quietly, she slipped out of bed and tiptoed to the living room. Emma had a small collection of books on a shelf, and Lexi picked one at random, hoping a story might distract her. She settled onto the couch, the soft glow of a lamp casting comforting shadows.

The book helped, a little. She lost herself in the narrative, the words a temporary escape from her fear. But as the night wore on and the city outside began to stir, she couldn't shake the feeling that this was only the beginning. The masked figure, the note—they were harbingers of something darker, something she couldn't yet understand.

Morning came, bringing a sense of clarity. Lexi knew she couldn't live in fear, and couldn't let this unknown threat control her life. She needed answers, and she needed to take action.

Emma was already up, making breakfast. She smiled as Lexi entered the kitchen. "How did you sleep?" Lexi shrugged. "Not great. But I've been thinking. I need to figure out who this person is and why they're targeting me."

Emma nodded, setting a plate of pancakes on the table. "Agreed. And I'll help you. We'll get through this together."

As they ate, they made a plan. Lexi would talk to her contacts at Bellevue Manor, to see if anyone had seen anything unusual. They'd also look into recent events in the city, and see if there were any patterns or clues.

But most importantly, Lexi wouldn't let fear rule her life. She had friends who cared about her, a job she loved, and a determination to uncover the truth.

The day ahead was daunting, the road uncertain. But with Emma by her side and a resolve to find answers, Lexi felt a glimmer of hope. She would face this threat head-on, and she wouldn't rest until she knew the truth.

As they finished breakfast and prepared to face the day, Lexi couldn't help but feel a sense of determination. The masked figure might be watching, but she wouldn't let them win. She would find them, and she would uncover their secrets.

The game was on, and Lexi Thompson was ready to play.

So there you have it, another night of fear and confusion for our heroine. But don't worry, Lexi's not the type to back down easily. She's got a fire in her that no masked figure can extinguish.

CHAPTER THREE

SHADOWS OF THE PAST

Hey, let's take a step back. Ever wondered why Lexi is the way she is? Why does she keep everyone at arm's length, no matter how close they try to get?

Lexi Thompson, her hair still damp from the shower, stared at her reflection in Emma's bathroom mirror. Dark circles under her eyes and a pallor to her usually vibrant complexion told the story of a sleepless night. She rubbed her temples, trying to shake off the lingering unease. The past few days had been a whirlwind of fear and confusion, but beneath it all was an even deeper scar, one that had shaped her long before the masked figure appeared.

Let's rewind to a time when Lexi wasn't just Lexi the event planner. She was Lexi, the dreamer, the romantic. Central Park in the fall, leaves a fiery tapestry underfoot, and there she was, hand in hand with Alexander. They were the couple everyone envied, the kind you see in movies and think, "That's what love looks like."

"Lex, you ever think about our future?" Alexander had asked one crisp afternoon, his eyes sparkling with that mischievous glint she adored.

"Every day," she replied, leaning into him, feeling his warmth. "I want it all, Alex. The house, the kids, the whole fairy tale."

He had laughed, that rich, infectious sound that could brighten her darkest days. "You'll get your fairy tale, Lexi. I promise."

But promises are just words until they're broken, aren't they?

Fast forward to a year later. SoHo is the heart of art and culture, where Lexi and Alexander had their favorite café. They'd spent countless hours there, planning their future, lost in each other. But this time, the conversation wasn't about dreams and tomorrows. It was about betrayal.

"Lexi, I... I don't know how to say this," Alexander had begun, his voice shaky, eyes avoiding hers.

She knew. Oh, she knew. You see, when you love someone, truly love them, you notice everything. The late nights at work, the sudden distance, the unfamiliar perfume on his clothes. It all added up to one undeniable truth.

"There's someone else, isn't there?" Her voice had been barely a whisper, the weight of her suspicion finally crashing down.

Alexander had nodded, tears in his eyes. "I never meant to hurt you. It just happened."

Lexi had felt her heart shatter into a million pieces. The fairy tale was over, replaced by a harsh, unforgiving reality. She had walked out of the café, leaving behind the man she thought she'd spend forever with, her dreams turning to dust in the wind.

Now, standing in Emma's bathroom, Lexi couldn't help but reflect on how those experiences had shaped her. She had built walls, strong and high, around her heart. Trust was no longer freely given; it had to be earned. Love, once an open invitation, had become a guarded secret.

Emma's voice pulled her from her thoughts. "Lexi, breakfast is ready!"

Taking a deep breath, Lexi forced a smile and stepped out into the warmth of Emma's kitchen. The smell of pancakes and fresh coffee filled the air, a small comfort in an otherwise tumultuous world.

"Morning," Emma greeted, her voice cheerful. "Sleep any better?"

"Not really," Lexi admitted, taking a seat. "But I'm determined to get to the bottom of this."

Emma nodded, placing a stack of pancakes in front of her. "We will. But first, eat. You need your strength."

Lexi picked at her food, her mind drifting back to those days with Alexander. They had been so in love, so sure of their future. But love, she had learned, was fragile. One misstep, one betrayal, and it could crumble, leaving nothing but heartache in its wake.

Flashback to another time, another place. A winter's day in the city, the air crisp and cold. Lexi and Alexander were ice skating at Rockefeller Center, laughing as they glided across the ice. It was a perfect moment, one of many they had shared.

"Careful, Lexi!" Alexander had called, just as she stumbled. But he was there, catching her before she fell. "Gotcha," he whispered, his breath warm against her ear.

She had looked up at him, their faces inches apart, and felt that familiar flutter in her chest. "I love you," she had said, the words so easy, so natural.

"I love you too," he had replied, sealing it with a kiss.

But love, as she had learned, was not enough to hold them together. The cracks had appeared slowly, almost imperceptibly, until one day, everything fell apart. And Lexi was left picking up the pieces of her broken heart, trying to make sense of it all.

"Lexi, you okay?" Emma's voice brought her back to the present.

"Yeah, just lost in thought," Lexi replied, forcing a smile.

Emma reached across the table, squeezing her hand. "We'll get through this. I promise."

Lexi nodded, grateful for her friend's support. She had learned to be wary of promises, but Emma's felt different. Solid. Trustworthy.

After breakfast, they decided to take a walk. The fresh air might do Lexi some good, and help clear her mind. They strolled through Brooklyn Heights, the streets quiet in the early morning light. As they walked, Lexi couldn't help but think about the parallels between her past and present. The masked figure, the notes, the sense of being watched—it all felt like a sinister echo of what she had been through with Alexander.

Another flashback, this time to a summer evening. Lexi and Alexander were at a rooftop bar, the city spread out below them, twinkling in the twilight. They were celebrating her promotion, toasting their bright future.

"To us," Alexander had said, raising his glass.

"To us," Lexi had echoed, feeling on top of the world.

But that world had come crashing down soon after. She had found out about his affair a few weeks later, the betrayal cutting deeper than any wound. She had confronted him, her heart breaking as he confessed. It had been the end of their relationship, but the beginning of a long journey for Lexi—a journey of remediation, of learning to trust again.

Now, as she walked with Emma, Lexi realized just how far she had come. She had built a successful career, surrounded herself with good friends, and learned to stand on her own two feet. But the scars of her past still lingered, affecting her in ways she didn't always understand.

They reached the park, finding a quiet bench to sit on. The morning sun filtered through the trees, casting dappled shadows on the ground.

"Lexi, I know you're scared," Emma said gently. "But you're not alone. We'll figure this out."

Lexi nodded, taking a deep breath. "I know. It's just… hard, you know? Trusting people, letting them in."

Emma squeezed her hand. "You're one of the strongest people I know. You've been through so much, and you've come out the other side. This masked figure, whoever they are, doesn't stand a chance against you."

Lexi smiled, feeling a glimmer of hope. She wasn't alone. She had friends who cared about her, and who would stand by her no matter what. And that was a powerful thing.

As they sat there, Lexi made a promise to herself. She would face this threat head-on, just as she had faced every challenge before. She wouldn't let fear control her life. She would find the masked figure, uncover the truth, and reclaim her sense of safety.

That night, back at Emma's apartment, Lexi felt a strange sense of calm. She knew the road ahead would be tough, but she was ready for it. She had faced betrayal, heartache, and fear before. She had come out stronger each time, and this would be no different.

As she lay in bed, the events of the past few days replayed in her mind. The masked figure, the notes, the feeling of being watched—it all pointed to something deeper, something she needed to understand.

She thought about Alexander, about the lessons she had learned from their relationship. Trust was fragile, but it was also essential. She needed to trust herself, to believe in her strength and resilience.

With that thought, she drifted off to sleep, feeling a sense of determination she hadn't felt in a long time. The masked figure might be a shadow from her past, but she was ready to face it. She was ready to reclaim her life.

CHAPTER FOUR

THE INTERVIEW

Okay, it's time for Lexi's world to collide with someone who could change everything. Imagine this a towering skyscraper, sleek and imposing, the kind that screams power and mystery. That's Blackwood Tower for you. And inside? Well, that's where Lexi's about to meet a man who's as enigmatic as he is charming.

Lexi Thompson, feeling a mix of nerves and excitement, stepped out of the cab and craned her neck to take in the full height of Blackwood Tower. The building loomed above her, a testament to modern architecture with its reflective glass and steel façade. She adjusted her blazer, took a deep breath, and walked through the revolving doors into the lobby, her heels clicking against the marble floor.

The lobby was a testament to opulence, with high ceilings, polished stone, and an array of contemporary art pieces adorning the walls. She approached the reception desk, where a young woman with a friendly smile greeted her.

"Good morning, how can I help you?" the receptionist asked.

"I have an appointment with Mr. Blackwood," Lexi replied, trying to keep her voice steady.

The receptionist nodded and checked her computer. "Of course, Ms. Thompson. Please take the elevator to the 40th floor. His assistant, Rachel, will meet you there."

Lexi thanked her and made her way to the elevator. As the doors closed and the elevator began its ascent, she couldn't help but feel a flutter of anticipation. Beckett Blackwood was a name synonymous with success, wealth, and mystery. What would he be like in person?

The elevator doors opened to reveal a spacious, elegantly decorated floor. Rachel, a poised and efficient-looking woman in her early thirties, greeted her with a warm smile.

"Ms. Thompson, welcome. Please follow me," Rachel said, leading her down a corridor lined with tasteful artwork. They reached a set of double doors, which Rachel opened with a soft knock. "Mr. Blackwood, Ms. Thompson is here for her interview."

"Thank you, Rachel," a deep, smooth voice responded from within.

Lexi stepped into the room and immediately felt the intensity of Beckett Blackwood's presence. He stood by the window, his back to her, gazing out at the city below. Tall and broad-shouldered, he exuded a quiet power. He turned slowly, and Lexi found herself looking into a pair of strikingly blue eyes that seemed to see right through her.

"Ms. Thompson," he said, extending his hand. "Thank you for coming."

She shook his hand, noting the firm grip. "Thank you for having me, Mr. Blackwood."

"Please, call me Beckett. Have a seat," he said, gesturing to the chair opposite his desk.

Lexi sat down, trying to steady her nerves. Beckett Blackwood was even more imposing in person, with his chiseled features and the kind of confidence that came from years of being at the top.

Their conversation began with the usual formalities—her background, and her experience in event planning.

But it wasn't long before Beckett's questions took a more personal turn.

"Why did you choose this field, Lexi?" he asked, leaning back in his chair, fingers steep led under his chin.

She hesitated, then decided to be honest. "I've always loved creating memorable experiences for people. There's something magical about bringing a vision to life and seeing the joy it brings to others."

He nodded, seemingly satisfied with her answer. "And what do you do when things don't go as planned?"

Lexi smiled, a hint of her determination shining through. "I adapt. No event ever goes perfectly, but it's my job to make sure no one else notices when something goes wrong."

Beckett's eyes narrowed slightly as if he were assessing her. "And what about challenges outside of work? How do you handle those?"

Lexi felt a pang in her chest, memories of Alexander flashing through her mind. "I face them head-on," she said quietly. "I've learned that running away doesn't solve anything."

Their conversation continued, Beckett's questions growing more probing, more personal. Lexi found herself opening up in a way she hadn't expected. There was something about him, an intensity that drew her in and made her want to reveal more.

But she couldn't shake the feeling that Beckett was hiding something too. His eyes, though piercing, held a hint of sadness, a shadow of something unspoken.

Rachel reappeared, interrupting their conversation. "Mr. Blackwood, your next appointment is in ten minutes."

Beckett nodded. "Thank you, Rachel." He turned back to Lexi. "This has been... enlightening. I'll have Rachel be in touch with the details if we decide to move forward."

Lexi stood, extending her hand once more. "Thank you for your time, Beckett."

He shook her hand, his touch lingering just a moment longer than necessary. "Thank you, Lexi. I look forward to seeing what you can do."

As she left Blackwood Tower, Lexi felt a strange mix of emotions. Beckett Blackwood was unlike anyone she had ever met. Charismatic, yes, but also enigmatic, his true self hidden behind a carefully constructed façade.

The city bustled around her, but Lexi's mind was still in that office, replaying their conversation. She sensed that Beckett was testing her, pushing her to reveal her true self. And she couldn't help but wonder—what was he hiding? What secrets lay behind those piercing blue eyes?

That night, back in the safety of her apartment, Lexi reflected on the day's events. She had met powerful clients before, but none had left such an impression on her. There was a magnetism to Beckett that was hard to ignore, but also a wariness, as if he was constantly on guard.

She thought about the masked figure, the unsettling occurrences, and now this enigmatic billionaire who seemed to see right through her. It was all connected, she was sure of it. But how? And what did it mean for her?

The next morning, Lexi woke with a renewed sense of determination. She was going to uncover the truth, whatever it took. She couldn't let fear control her life, and she certainly wasn't going to let anyone—masked figure or billionaire—intimidate her.

She called Emma, filling her in on the details of the interview. "He's... intense," she said, trying to find the right words.

Emma laughed. "Intense? Lexi, you just met one of the most powerful men in the city. Of course, he's intense."

"But there's more to him, Emma. I can feel it. He's hiding something."

"Maybe, but that's not your concern right now. Focus on the job. If he hires you, show him what you're capable of. The rest will come."

Lexi knew her friend was right. She needed to stay focused, to prove herself. But she couldn't shake the feeling that Beckett Blackwood was going to be a bigger part of her life than she had anticipated.

Later that day, Rachel called with the news that she had been hired. Lexi felt a thrill of excitement mixed with a touch of apprehension. She was about to enter Beckett's world, a world of luxury, power, and secrets.

Her first event was a charity gala at Blackwood Tower, and she threw herself into the preparations with fervor.

She worked late into the night, pouring over details, and making sure everything was perfect. This was her chance to prove herself, and she wasn't going to let it slip away.

The night of the gala arrived, and Lexi felt a mix of nerves and excitement. She stood at the entrance, greeting guests, her eyes constantly scanning the room for any sign of trouble. Beckett was there, of course, looking every bit the powerful billionaire. He moved through the crowd with ease, charming everyone he spoke to.

But Lexi couldn't help but notice the way his eyes occasionally drifted to her, watching her with an intensity that made her heart race. She felt a strange connection to him, a pull that she couldn't quite explain.

As the night wore on, she found herself drawn to him, their paths crossing more than once. Each time, there was a spark, an unspoken understanding that passed between them. She could see the sadness in his eyes, the shadows that he tried so hard to hide. Towards the end of the evening, Beckett approached her. "You've done an amazing job, Lexi," he said, his voice warm.

"Thank you," she replied, feeling a blush rise to her cheeks.

He looked at her, really looked at her, as if trying to see past the professional façade she wore. "Can I ask you something?"

"Of course," she said, her heart beating faster. "Why do you do this? Why event planning?"

She hesitated, then decided to be honest. "Because I love creating moments that people will remember. It's not just about the decorations or the food; it's about the experience and the emotions. I want to give people something they'll never forget."

Beckett nodded, a thoughtful expression on his face. "And what about your moments? What do you remember?"

Lexi felt a pang in her chest. Memories of Alexander, of heartbreak, of betrayal. "I remember… everything," she said quietly. "The good and the bad."

He looked at her for a long moment, then nodded. "I understand". As the night came to an end and the last guests left, Lexi found herself alone with Beckett. The room was quiet, the city lights twinkling outside the windows.

"Thank you for tonight," Beckett said, his voice soft. "You've done an incredible job."

Lexi smiled, feeling a warmth spread through her. "It was my pleasure."

They stood there in silence for a moment, the air between them charged with unspoken words. Lexi felt a pull towards him, a desire to understand the man behind the mask.

"Beckett, can I ask you something?" she said, breaking the silence.

"Anything," he replied, his eyes meeting hers. "What are you hiding?"

He looked at her, a flicker of surprise in his eyes. Then he sighed, running a hand through his hair. "I have my reasons, Lexi. There are things in my past... things I'm not proud of".

She stepped closer, her heart pounding. "We all have our secrets. But you don't have to carry them alone."

He looked at her, a mixture of gratitude and sadness in his eyes. "Thank you, Lexi. But some things are better left in the shadows."

As she left Blackwood Tower that night, Lexi felt a strange sense of connection to Beckett. He was a man of many layers, and she was determined to peel them back, one by one. She knew it wouldn't be easy, but she was ready for the challenge.

Her life was already complicated enough with the mysterious figure stalking her, but Beckett Blackwood had awakened something in her—a desire to trust again, to open her heart. And maybe, just maybe, he was the key to unlocking her shadows.

CHAPTER FIVE

THE MYSTERIOUS MR. BLACKWOOD

Lexi Thompson sat cross-legged on her couch, her laptop balanced on her knees. Her apartment in Brooklyn Heights was small but charming, filled with personal touches that made it homey. It was a stark contrast to the opulence of Blackwood Tower, where she had spent the past few days immersed in preparations for the charity gala. Tonight, however, her focus was entirely on Beckett Blackwood.

The gala had been a success, no doubt about it, but it wasn't just the professional satisfaction that had kept Lexi's mind whirling. It was Beckett. His presence, his questions, his enigmatic aura—they had all left a mark on her. She couldn't stop thinking about him, about the sadness in his eyes and the secrets he hinted at but didn't reveal.

"Okay, Lexi," she murmured to herself, adjusting her glasses. "Time to do some digging."

She started with the basics: a Google search of Beckett Blackwood. Predictably, the first results were a slew of business articles and profiles in glossy magazines. Forbes, Business Insider, and The Wall Street Journal—all heralding him as a financial genius, a visionary, and a titan of industry. His company, Blackwood Enterprises, had its fingers in countless pies: real estate, technology, and luxury goods. The man was everywhere.

But Lexi wasn't looking for the surface-level stuff. She wanted the story behind the story. The man behind the mask. She clicked through articles, looking for anything that might give her a glimpse of the real Beckett Blackwood.

In one interview, he spoke about his early days, growing up in a small town before moving to New York City. But the details were sparse, almost deliberately so. He mentioned his parents briefly—a father who had died when he was young, and a mother who had raised him alone. There was no mention of friends, no anecdotes about childhood. Just a relentless focus on his rise to power. A profile in Vanity Fair caught her eye. It painted Beckett as a solitary figure, driven by a need to prove himself. He was described as intensely private, rarely seen at social events unless they were for business. There were rumors, of course—whispers of affairs with models and actresses, but nothing ever confirmed.

Lexi's curiosity deepened. She found a few mentions of charity work, particularly a foundation he had established in his mother's name. But even here, the details were scant. It was clear Beckett preferred to keep his personal life out of the spotlight.

She leaned back, chewing on the end of a pencil. There had to be more. Something that explained the sadness she saw in his eyes, the weight he seemed to carry. She opened a new tab and began searching more creatively, using terms like "Beckett Blackwood scandal" and "Beckett Blackwood controversy."

It didn't take long to find something. An old article from a local newspaper buried deep in the search results mentioned a legal dispute involving Blackwood Enterprises and a former partner. The details were vague, but it hinted at a betrayal, a falling out that had nearly brought the company to its knees. Beckett had emerged victorious, of course, but at what cost?

Lexi's mind raced. Was this the source of his guarded nature? The reason he seemed so closed off? She made a mental note to look into it further. For now, she had enough to ponder.

As she continued her research, a knock at her door startled her. She looked up, momentarily disoriented, then set her laptop aside and went to answer it. Her friend Emma stood on the other side, holding a bottle of wine.

"Hey, Lex," Emma said with a grin. "Thought you might need a break."

Lexi laughed, stepping aside to let her in. "You have perfect timing. I was just getting sucked into the rabbit hole."

Emma raised an eyebrow. "The Beckett Blackwood rabbit hole?"

"Is it that obvious?" Lexi asked, grabbing two glasses from the kitchen. Emma poured the wine and handed a glass to Lexi. "You've been talking about him nonstop since the gala. Can you blame me for being curious?" Lexi took a sip, savoring the rich flavor. "He's... fascinating. There's so much more to him than meets the eye."

Emma settled onto the couch, looking intrigued. "Okay, spill. What have you found out?"

Lexi filled her in on the basics—the business empire, the charity work, the hints of a troubled past. Emma listened attentively, her expression thoughtful.

"So, he's a mysterious billionaire with a tragic backstory. Sounds like something out of a romance novel," Emma said with a smirk.

Lexi rolled her eyes. "It's not like that. I mean, yes, he's attractive and all, but it's more than that. I feel like there's a connection between us. Like he understands me in a way no one else does."

Emma's smirk softened into a sympathetic smile. "Lexi, you've been through a lot. It's natural to be drawn to someone who seems to get you. Just... be careful, okay? These billionaire types can be complicated." I know," Lexi said, feeling a pang of doubt. "But I can't shake the feeling that there's something important I'm missing. Something I need to understand."

Emma reached over and squeezed her hand. "Then keep digging. Just don't lose yourself in the process."

After Emma left, Lexi returned to her laptop, her mind buzzing with thoughts. She felt a renewed determination to uncover the truth about Beckett Blackwood. She needed to understand him, to see beyond the façade he presented to the world.

The next few days were a blur of work and research. Lexi threw herself into her event planning duties, but in every spare moment, she was back at her laptop, piecing together the puzzle that was Beckett Blackwood.

One evening, as she sifted through old articles and obscure forum posts, she stumbled upon a name that kept appearing—Jonathan Hargrove. He was mentioned in connection with the legal dispute, and there were hints that he and Beckett had once been close friends and business partners.

Intrigued, Lexi dug deeper. She found an old photo of the two men, standing side by side at a company event. Beckett looked younger, less guarded, his smile more genuine. Jonathan, on the other hand, had a sharp, calculating look, a contrast to Beckett's easy charm.

The more she read, the more she realized that Jonathan Hargrove might hold the key to understanding Beckett's past. But finding out more about him proved difficult. He had dropped out of the public eye after the legal dispute, his whereabouts unknown.

Lexi sat back, frustration gnawing at her. She needed more information, but she wasn't sure where to turn next. Then an idea struck her—Rachel. Beckett's assistant was bound to know something. She just had to find a way to get Rachel to open up.

The next morning, Lexi arrived at Blackwood Tower early, hoping to catch Rachel before the day's meetings began. She spotted her in the lobby, carrying a stack of files.

"Rachel, hi!" Lexi called, hurrying over.

Rachel looked up, a bit surprised. "Lexi, good morning. What brings you here so early?"

Lexi flashed her best smile. "I was hoping to catch you for a quick coffee before things get busy. I wanted to pick your brain about a few things."

Rachel hesitated, then nodded. "Sure, I have a few minutes. Let's head to the café." They settled into a corner table at the nearby café, steaming cups of coffee in front of them. Lexi decided to ease into the conversation, starting with small talk about the gala and upcoming events.

"You've been working with Mr. Blackwood for a while, right?" Lexi asked casually.

Rachel nodded. "Yes, almost five years now. He's a brilliant man, but very private."

Lexi leaned forward slightly. "I've noticed that. There's so much I want to understand about him, but he's hard to read."

Rachel gave her a curious look. "Why the sudden interest?"

Lexi hesitated, then decided to be honest. "I feel like there's more to him than meets the eye. He's been through a lot, hasn't he?"

Rachel sighed, stirring her coffee. "He has. The thing about Beckett is, he's been hurt before. He doesn't trust easily."

Lexi's heart ached at the thought. "What happened with Jonathan Hargrove? They seemed so close in the old photos."

Rachel's expression darkened. "Jonathan was Beckett's best friend and business partner. But he betrayed Beckett in the worst way. It nearly destroyed the company."

Lexi felt a chill run down her spine. "What did he do?"

Rachel glanced around, lowering her voice. "He embezzled money and made bad deals behind Beckett's back. When Beckett found out, he was devastated. They had been like brothers."

Lexi's mind whirled. No wonder Beckett was so guarded, so wary of letting anyone get too close. "That must have been incredibly hard for him."

"It was," Rachel agreed. "But he rebuilt the company, stronger than ever. He's resilient, but he's also put up walls to protect himself."

As Lexi walked back to Blackwood Tower, Rachel's words echoed in her mind. Beckett had been betrayed by someone he trusted implicitly. It explained so much about his behavior, and his reluctance to open up. She felt a deep empathy for him, a desire to help him heal those old wounds.

Later that evening, back in her apartment, Lexi sat at her desk, reflecting on everything she had learned. Her feelings for Beckett were growing stronger, but so was her determination to understand him. She knew it wouldn't be easy, but she was willing to try.

She opened her laptop and began writing a letter, pouring out her thoughts and emotions. She didn't know if she would ever give it to him, but it helped to put her feelings into words.

"Dear Beckett,

I know you've been through a lot, and I can't pretend to understand everything you've experienced. But I want you to know that you're not alone. You don't have to carry your burdens by yourself. I see you, the real you, behind the walls you've built. And I want to be there for you if you'll let me.

Yours, Lexi"

She read the letter over, feeling a mixture of hope and uncertainty. Beckett was a complicated man, and she knew this journey wouldn't be straightforward. But she was willing to take the risk, to open her heart and see where it led.

CHAPTER SIX

THE UNEXPECTED ENCOUNTER

The air in SoHo was electric, buzzing with the energy of artists, fashionistas, and those simply looking to soak in the vibe of New York City's trendiest neighborhood. Lexi had always loved this part of town—the quirky boutiques, the street art, the eclectic mix of people. Today, she decided to take a break from her relentless work schedule and indulge in some much-needed downtime.

She pushed open the door of her favorite coffee shop, a small, artsy place tucked away on a side street. The smell of freshly ground coffee beans mingled with the sweet scent of pastries, instantly lifting her spirits. She approached the counter, greeted by the familiar barista who knew her usual order by heart.

"Hey, Lexi! The usual?" he asked with a grin.

"Joe. Extra shot of espresso, please," she replied, returning his smile.

As she waited for her coffee, Lexi scanned the room, her eyes landing on a familiar face sitting at a corner table. Her heart skipped a beat. Beckett Blackwood. Of all the places in New York City, he was here, in her favorite coffee shop. He looked different in this setting—more relaxed, less guarded. He was engrossed in a book, a small smile playing on his lips.

For a moment, Lexi considered slipping out quietly, avoiding the encounter. But something stopped her. Maybe it was the curiosity that had been gnawing at her since their last meeting, or perhaps it was the letter she had written but never sent. Either way, she found herself moving towards him. "Beckett?" she said softly, hoping she wasn't interrupting.

He looked up, surprise flickering across his face before it was replaced by a warm smile. "Lexi. What a pleasant surprise."

She felt a flutter in her chest at his words. "Mind if I join you?"

"Please, have a seat," he said, motioning to the chair opposite him.

Joe brought her coffee, giving her a knowing look before retreating to the counter. Lexi took a sip, savoring the rich flavor as she tried to calm her racing heart.

"So, what brings you to SoHo?" she asked, genuinely curious.

Beckett closed his book, setting it aside. "I needed a change of scenery. Sometimes, the office can feel a bit... suffocating."

Lexi nodded, understanding all too well. "I get that. This place is my little escape from reality."

They fell into an easy conversation, talking about everything from their favorite books to the best hidden gems in the city. Lexi found herself laughing more than she had in weeks, charmed by Beckett's wit and intelligence. It was easy to forget who he was—the billionaire, the enigmatic figure—and just see him as a man who shared her love for the simple joys in life.

As the afternoon wore on, Lexi began to notice subtle changes in Beckett's demeanor. He leaned in closer, his eyes lingering on hers a little longer. There was a warmth in his gaze, a softness that she hadn't seen before.

"Lexi," he said, his voice low and sincere. "I've been thinking about you. A lot."

Her heart skipped a beat. "You have?"

He nodded, reaching across the table to take her hand. "I know this might seem sudden, but I feel a connection with you. Something I haven't felt in a long time."

Lexi's mind raced. She had felt it too, that undeniable pull towards him. But she couldn't forget who he was, the walls he had built around himself. "Beckett, I... I don't know."

He gave her hand a gentle squeeze. "I understand. But I'm willing to take a chance if you are. Let me show you who I am, beyond the headlines and the money."

Lexi's breath caught in her throat. This was the moment she had been hoping for, yet it terrified her. She wanted to believe in him, to let herself fall. But could she?

"All right," she said finally, her voice barely above a whisper. "But let's take it slow."

Beckett's smile was radiant, filling her with a warmth she hadn't felt in a long time. "Slow sounds perfect."

Over the next few days, Beckett made good on his promise. He invited Lexi to dinner at an intimate restaurant in the West Village, a place with dim lighting and soft jazz playing in the background. The atmosphere was cozy and romantic, and as they shared a bottle of wine, Lexi felt herself relaxing, letting her guard down.

They talked for hours, sharing stories and dreams. Beckett revealed more about his past, the struggles he had faced, and the people who had shaped him. Lexi listened, her heart aching for the boy he had been, admiring the man he had become.

One evening, he took her to a private gallery opening, a charity event for the foundation he had established in his mother's name. Lexi was awed by the art, and the talent on display, but more so by the way Beckett interacted with the artists, the genuine interest and support he showed them.

"He's amazing, isn't he?" a voice said beside her.

Lexi turned to see an older woman, elegantly dressed, her eyes warm with affection. "Yes, he is," Lexi replied, feeling a swell of pride.

"I've known Beckett for years," the woman continued. "He has a good heart, but it's been bruised. Be patient with him. He's worth it."

Lexi smiled, touched by the woman's words. "Thank you. I'll remember that."

As the weeks passed, Beckett and Lexi grew closer, their bond deepening with each shared moment. He was attentive, and considerate, always finding ways to make her feel special. Yet, there were still moments when she saw a shadow cross his face, a flicker of something unresolved.

One evening, as they walked along the Hudson River, Beckett took her hand, his expression serious. "Lexi, there's something I need to tell you."

Her heart pounded in her chest. "What is it?"

He took a deep breath, his grip tightening on her hand. "My past... it's complicated. There are things I haven't told you. Things I'm not proud of."

Lexi's pulse quickened, but she met his gaze steadily. "Whatever it is, you can tell me. I'm here for you, Beckett."

He looked away, staring out at the water. "Jonathan Hargrove wasn't just a business partner. He was my best friend. We started the company together and built it from the ground up. But he betrayed me, in ways I can't even begin to explain. It nearly destroyed everything I had worked for."

Lexi squeezed his hand, her heart aching for him. "I'm so sorry, Beckett. That must have been incredibly painful."

"It was," he admitted, his voice thick with emotion. "But it wasn't just the betrayal. It was what came after. The legal battles, and the media frenzy. I lost a part of myself during that time. I became someone I didn't recognize."

Lexi felt tears prick her eyes. She reached up, cupping his face in her hands. "You're not that person anymore. You've come so far, and you're still here, still fighting."

Beckett leaned into her touch, closing his eyes. "You make me want to be better, Lexi. To let go of the past and move forward."

They stood there, holding each other, the city lights reflecting off the water. At that moment, Lexi knew she was falling in love with Beckett Blackwood. It was terrifying and exhilarating all at once. She didn't know what the future held, but she was willing to take the risk, to face the challenges together.

The next morning, Beckett surprised her with a weekend getaway to a secluded cabin upstate. It was a world away from the hustle and bustle of the city, a place where they could truly be alone. Lexi was touched by the gesture, by the effort he was making to show her his world, to build something real with her.

They spent the days hiking through the woods, exploring the natural beauty around them. At night, they curled up by the fireplace, sharing stories and dreams, their connection growing stronger with each passing moment.

One evening, as they sat on the porch, watching the stars, Beckett turned to her, his eyes filled with a vulnerability she hadn't seen before.

"Lexi, I know I've asked a lot of you, and I know this isn't easy. But I need you to know that I'm serious about us. I want to build a future with you."

Lexi's heart swelled with emotion. "I want that too, Beckett. More than anything."

He reached into his pocket, pulling out a small, intricately carved wooden box. "I know it's still early, but I want you to have this. It's a promise, a symbol of my commitment to you."

Lexi opened the box, revealing a delicate silver necklace, a single diamond pendant catching the light. She felt tears welling up in her eyes. "It's beautiful, Beckett. Thank you."

He fastened the necklace around her neck, his fingers lingering on her skin. "I love you, Lexi."

She looked into his eyes, her heart overflowing with love and gratitude. "I love you too, Beckett."

CHAPTER SEVEN

THE PROPOSITION

The view from Beckett's penthouse was nothing short of breathtaking. Floor-to-ceiling windows framed the glittering skyline of Manhattan, the city lights twinkling like a thousand tiny stars. The room itself was a masterpiece of modern design—sleek lines, minimalist decor, and every conceivable luxury. It was the kind of place that made you feel both awed and slightly out of place.

Lexi stood by the window, her heart racing. She had been here before, of course, but tonight felt different. Tonight, there was an edge to Beckett's demeanor, a sense of anticipation that made her nervous.

"Lexi," Beckett's voice was soft, yet commanding, as he joined her by the window. "There's something I need to discuss with you."

She turned to face him, her eyes searching his. "What is it, Beckett?" He took a deep breath, his gaze never leaving hers. "I've been thinking a lot about us, about our future. I want you to be a part of my life, in every possible way."

Lexi's heart skipped a beat. "What do you mean?"

Beckett reached out, taking her hands in his. "I want you to become my assistant. Officially. It would mean working closely with me, traveling, being involved in all aspects of my business and personal life."

Lexi's mind raced. It was an incredible offer, one that came with unimaginable perks and opportunities. But it also meant blurring the lines between their professional and personal lives, stepping deeper into his world—a world that could be both dazzling and dangerous.

"I don't know, Beckett. It's a lot to consider," she said, her voice trembling slightly.

He squeezed her hands, his eyes earnest. "I know it's a big ask, but I trust you, Lexi. More than anyone. I need someone by my side who understands me, someone I can rely on completely."

Lexi looked out at the city, her thoughts swirling. She had worked so hard to build her career, to establish herself as an independent woman. But the prospect of being with Beckett, of sharing his world, was incredibly tempting.

"What about my event planning business?" she asked, her voice barely above a whisper.

Beckett smiled a hint of mischief in his eyes. "We can figure that out. I have resources and connections. We can make it work. You wouldn't have to give up your dreams, Lexi. If anything, this could open even more doors for you."

She bit her lip, weighing her options. The rational part of her screamed caution, but her heart... her heart wanted to leap. She looked back at Beckett, seeing the hope and vulnerability in his eyes.

"All right," she said finally, her voice steady. "I'll do it. I'll be your assistant."

The relief that washed over Beckett's face was palpable. He pulled her into his arms, holding her tightly. "Thank you, Lexi. You won't regret this, I promise."

As they embraced, Lexi felt a mix of emotions—excitement, fear, anticipation. This was a new chapter, a bold step into the unknown. She could only hope that it would lead to something wonderful.

The next morning, Lexi woke up in Beckett's penthouse, sunlight streaming through the windows. She stretched, feeling a sense of calm despite the whirlwind of emotions from the night before. She had made her decision, and now it was time to embrace it.

Beckett was already up, sitting at the kitchen counter with a cup of coffee and a stack of papers. He looked up as she entered, a smile spreading across his face.

"Good morning, beautiful," he said, his voice warm.

"Good morning," she replied, joining him at the counter. "What's all this?"

"Just some contracts and paperwork for you to look over," he said, handing her a folder. "I want everything to be official and above board".

Lexi took the folder, flipping through the documents. It was all very professional, outlining her new role, responsibilities, and compensation. She couldn't help but be impressed by the thoroughness of it all.

As she signed the papers, Beckett watched her, his expression one of quiet admiration. "You're doing this," he said softly. "We're doing this".

She looked up, meeting his gaze. "Yes, we are. And I'm ready."

The days that followed were a whirlwind of activity. Lexi was introduced to Beckett's world in a way she had never imagined. She attended high-powered meetings, mingled with influential figures, and got a glimpse of the sheer magnitude of his empire. It was exhilarating and overwhelming, but through it all, Beckett was by her side, guiding her, supporting her.

One evening, they attended a charity gala at one of the city's most prestigious venues. Lexi felt like Cinderella, dressed in a stunning gown, her hair and makeup done to perfection. Beckett was the perfect gentleman, his arm around her waist as they mingled with the elite.

As they danced under the twinkling chandeliers, Beckett leaned in close, his breath warm against her ear. "You look incredible tonight," he whispered.

Lexi blushed, her heart fluttering. "Thank you. This is all a bit surreal."

He chuckled, pulling her closer. "Get used to it, my love. This is our life now."

As the music swelled around them, Lexi felt a sense of belonging, a feeling that she was exactly where she was meant to be.

But not everything was perfect. With the new role came new challenges. Lexi found herself constantly juggling her responsibilities, trying to balance her work with Beckett and her ambitions. It was a delicate dance, one that required patience and understanding from both of them.

One afternoon, as they sat in Beckett's office, Lexi could sense a tension in the air. He was engrossed in his work, his brow furrowed in concentration. She approached him, placing a hand on his shoulder.

"Is everything okay?" she asked gently.

Beckett sighed, running a hand through his hair. "Just some issues with a new project. It's nothing you need to worry about."

Lexi frowned, sensing there was more to it. "Beckett, you can talk to me. I'm here for you."

He looked up, his eyes softening. "I know. It's just... sometimes I feel like I'm juggling a thousand things at once. And I don't want to burden you with my problems."

She knelt beside him, taking his hand in hers. "You're not burdening me. We're in this together, remember? Whatever it is, we'll face it together."

He squeezed her hand, his expression grateful. "Thank you, Lexi. I don't know what I'd do without you."

As the weeks turned into months, Lexi and Beckett's relationship continued to deepen. They shared their dreams, their fears, and their secrets. Lexi learned more about Beckett's past, the struggles he had faced, and the demons he was still fighting. And in turn, Beckett became her rock, supporting her through the highs and lows of her journey.

One evening, as they sat on the rooftop terrace of the penthouse, Lexi looked out at the city, feeling a sense of contentment. Beckett wrapped his arms around her from behind, resting his chin on her shoulder.

"This city is beautiful," she said softly. "But it's even more beautiful with you. "He kissed her neck, his breath warm against her skin. "I feel the same way. You've brought so much light into my life, Lexi. I can't imagine it without you."

She turned to face him, her eyes shining with love. "I love you, Beckett. More than words can say".

He cupped her face in his hands, his gaze intense. "And I love you, Lexi. You're my everything".

As they kissed under the stars, Lexi knew that they were on the brink of something incredible. It wouldn't always be easy, and there would be challenges ahead. But together, they could face anything.

CHAPTER EIGHT

THE STALKER

Love isn't always roses and champagne; sometimes, shadows from the past creep in, threatening the fragile peace we've built.

The city's rhythm was intoxicating, a constant hum of life and energy. Lexi tried to immerse herself in it, to lose herself in the work and excitement that came with being Beckett's assistant. But a lingering sense of unease gnawed at her, like a shadow she couldn't shake.

It started with small things. A familiar car parked near her apartment, a bouquet of roses with no card. Lexi brushed them off as coincidences, refusing to let her mind wander back to Alexander. He was a part of her past—a dark chapter she had closed. Or so she thought.

One evening, after a long day at the office, Lexi decided to unwind with a walk through Central Park. The sun had just set, casting a golden glow over the city. She strolled along the pathways, breathing in the crisp air, trying to shake off the feeling that she was being watched.

Just as she reached a secluded bench, a voice from behind made her freeze. "Lexi."

Her heart pounded in her chest. She turned slowly, her worst fears confirmed. Alexander stood there, his eyes dark and intense, a twisted smile on his face.

"Alexander," she whispered, taking a step back. "What are you doing here?"

He took a step forward, closing the distance between them. "I've missed you, Lexi. We have unfinished business."

Lexi's mind raced. She needed to get away, to find safety. But the park was eerily empty, and Alexander's presence was suffocating.

"I don't want anything to do with you," she said, her voice shaking. "Leave me alone."

Alexander's smile faded, replaced by a menacing glare. "You don't get to walk away from me, Lexi. You belong to me. "Just as panic began to set in, a figure appeared from the shadows. Beckett. His presence was commanding, his expression steely.

"Is there a problem here?" Beckett's voice was calm but carried an edge of danger.

Alexander straightened, clearly recognizing Beckett. "This is none of your business, Blackwood."

Beckett stepped between them, his gaze never leaving Alexander. "I'm making it my business. Leave her alone."

For a moment, it seemed like Alexander might retaliate. But he hesitated, his eyes flickering with uncertainty. With a final glare at Lexi, he turned and walked away, disappearing into the night.

Lexi felt her knees buckle with relief. Beckett caught her, holding her close. "Are you all right?"

She nodded, tears streaming down her face. "Thank you, Beckett. I was so scared."

He stroked her hair gently, his touch soothing. "You're safe now, Lexi. I won't let anything happen to you."

Over the next few days, Beckett took every measure to ensure Lexi's safety. He assigned security to her apartment, installed high-tech surveillance, and even had his team dig into Alexander's background. Lexi was grateful, but the constant reminders of Alexander's presence left her on edge.

One evening, as they sat in Beckett's penthouse, Lexi voiced her fears. "I don't know how to escape him, Beckett. He's always been so… controlling."

Beckett took her hand, his expression serious. "We'll find a way, Lexi. I promise you. He won't hurt you again."

The next morning, Beckett's security team presented their findings. Alexander had a history of obsessive behavior, and multiple restraining orders from past girlfriends. He was dangerous, and they needed a plan.

"We'll take this to the authorities," Beckett said, his tone decisive. "With the evidence we have, they can issue a more severe restraining order."

Lexi nodded, feeling a glimmer of hope. "Thank you, Beckett. For everything."

He smiled, squeezing her hand. "You don't have to thank me. I care about you, Lexi. I won't let anyone harm you."

The following days were a blur of meetings with lawyers and police officers. Lexi recounted her history with Alexander, the abuse, the manipulation. It was painful but necessary. Beckett was with her every step of the way, his presence a constant source of strength.

One night, after a particularly exhausting day, Lexi collapsed onto the couch in Beckett's penthouse. He joined her, wrapping his arms around her.

"Are you okay?" he asked softly.

She nodded, leaning into him. "I'm just tired. But I feel... safer. With you."

Beckett kissed the top of her head. "You are safe, Lexi. And you always will be."

Weeks passed, and the legal process moved forward. Alexander was served with a restraining order, and the police kept a close watch on him. Lexi began to relax, slowly reclaiming her sense of normalcy. She threw herself into her work, finding solace in the bustling activity of the office and the projects she managed.

One afternoon, as she was finalizing details for an upcoming gala, Beckett walked into her office, a thoughtful expression on his face. "I've been thinking," he began, taking a seat across from her. "About us. About everything we've been through".

Lexi looked up, her heart skipping a beat. "What about it?"

He reached across the desk, taking her hand in his. "I want you to know how much you mean to me, Lexi. You've become an integral part of my life. More than just my assistant."

She felt a lump in her throat, overwhelmed by his sincerity. "I feel the same way, Beckett. You've been my rock through all of this".

He smiled, his eyes softening. "I don't want to lose you, Lexi. I want us to build a future together."

Lexi's heart swelled with emotion. "I'd like that. More than anything."

As they sat there, holding hands, a sense of peace washed over Lexi. Despite the challenges they faced, she knew they were stronger together. They had found each other in the chaos, and that was something worth holding onto.

The evening of the gala arrived, and Lexi found herself once again in a stunning gown, her hair and makeup done to perfection. Beckett was by her side, looking every bit the dashing billionaire. They arrived at the venue, the atmosphere buzzing with excitement.

As they mingled with the guests, Lexi couldn't help but feel a sense of pride. She had helped organize this event, and it was a resounding success. Beckett stayed close, his arm around her waist, introducing her to influential figures and praising her work.

At one point, as they stood by the bar, Beckett leaned in, his voice low. "I'm so proud of you, Lexi. You've handled everything with such grace and strength."

She smiled, her heart fluttering. "I couldn't have done it without you, Beckett. You've given me so much support."

He kissed her gently, their connection undeniable. "We make a great team, don't we?"

"We do," she agreed, feeling a warmth spread through her.

The night continued, filled with laughter, dancing, and celebration. For the first time in a long time, Lexi felt truly happy. She had faced her demons, with Beckett by her side, and come out stronger. They were building a future together, one filled with love, trust, and endless possibilities.

As the gala wound down and they returned to the penthouse, Lexi felt a sense of contentment. She and Beckett sat on the rooftop terrace, looking out at the city that never slept.

"Do you ever think about the future?" she asked, her voice soft.

Beckett nodded, his gaze thoughtful. "All the time. Especially now, with you."

She smiled, feeling a sense of excitement. "What do you see?"

He turned to her, his eyes filled with love. "I see us. Together. Happy. Maybe a family, if that's something you want."

Lexi's heart swelled with emotion. "I'd like that. More than anything."

As they sat there, wrapped in each other's arms, Lexi knew that they were on the brink of something incredible. Their journey had been filled with challenges, but together, they were unstoppable.

CHAPTER NINE

CROSSING BOUNDARIES

Yes, it's Lexi's first day as Beckett's assistant it was nothing short of overwhelming. The Blackwood Tower was an imposing structure, a testament to Beckett's wealth and power. The building's sleek, modern design exuded sophistication, and Lexi couldn't help but feel a mix of awe and trepidation as she walked through its polished glass doors.

Rachel, Beckett's primary assistant, greeted her with a warm smile. "Welcome to Blackwood Tower, Lexi. Beckett's waiting for you in his office."

"Thank you, Rachel," Lexi replied, trying to steady her nerves.

As they walked through the corridors, Lexi marveled at the art adorning the walls, each piece carefully curated. The offices buzzed with activity, everyone seeming to know their role in the well-oiled machine that was Beckett Blackwood's empire. Rachel knocked lightly on a large mahogany door before pushing it open. "Lexi's here," she announced.

Beckett looked up from his desk, his eyes lighting up as he saw her. "Lexi, come in. Have a seat."

Lexi crossed the room, her heels clicking softly on the marble floor. She took a seat opposite Beckett, trying to ignore the flutter in her stomach at his intense gaze.

"So, how are you feeling?" Beckett asked, his tone gentle.

"A bit nervous," Lexi admitted. "But excited too".

He smiled, a reassuring look that made her heart skip a beat. "You'll do great. Rachel will show you the ropes, and I'll be here if you need anything."

Lexi nodded, feeling a bit more at ease. "Thank you, Beckett. I appreciate the opportunity."

Rachel handed her a tablet, filled with schedules, contacts, and tasks. "This will be your lifeline," she said with a wink. "Don't worry, it looks like a lot, but you'll get the hang of it."

The day passed in a whirlwind of meetings, phone calls, and endless emails. Lexi quickly realized that Beckett's world was one of constant motion, where decisions had to be made in the blink of an eye and every detail mattered. Despite the hectic pace, she found herself

thriving, her skills as an event planner proving invaluable in managing the chaos.

During a brief lull, Beckett called her into his office. "How's it going?" he asked, his tone more relaxed than before.

"Good," Lexi replied, a bit breathless. "It's a lot, but I'm managing."

He leaned back in his chair, studying her. "I knew you would. You're incredibly capable, Lexi."

Their eyes met, and for a moment, the busy office around them seemed to fade away. Lexi felt a warmth spread through her, a connection that was becoming increasingly difficult to ignore.

As the weeks went by, Lexi settled into her new role. She and Beckett fell into a comfortable rhythm, their professional interactions tinged with a growing intimacy. Late nights at the office became a common occurrence, with Beckett often insisting on ordering dinner so they could continue working without interruption. One evening, after a particularly grueling day, Beckett suggested they take a break. "There's a rooftop terrace here with an amazing view. Want to join me?"

Lexi hesitated, aware of the boundaries they were constantly flirting with. But the prospect of some fresh air and a moment of relaxation was too tempting to pass up. "Sure, I'd love to."

The terrace was breathtaking, offering a panoramic view of the Manhattan skyline. The city lights glittered like stars, casting a magical glow over everything. Beckett handed her a glass of wine, and they stood side by side, taking in the view.

"This place is incredible," Lexi said, her voice soft with awe.

"It is," Beckett agreed, his eyes not on the city but on her. "I come up here when I need to clear my head."

Lexi took a sip of her wine, savoring the moment. "Thank you for bringing me up here."

He smiled, his gaze warm. "You deserve a break. You've been working so hard."

As they stood there, the air between them seemed to crackle with unspoken words and hidden desires. Lexi felt herself drawn to Beckett, the barriers she had carefully constructed beginning to crumble. But with

that attraction came uncertainty. Was this just a passing infatuation, or something more?

Their conversations became deeper, more personal. Beckett opened up about his past, the challenges he faced in building his empire, and the loneliness that often accompanied success. Lexi shared her struggles, her dreams, and the lingering fears that Alexander had left behind.

One night, after a particularly candid conversation, Beckett reached out and took her hand. "Lexi, I care about you. More than I probably should."

Lexi's heart raced, torn between her growing feelings for Beckett and the need to maintain her independence. "I care about you too, Beckett. But this... whatever this is between us... it's complicated." He nodded, understanding the dilemma. "I know. But I'm willing to navigate those complications if you are."

The line between professional and personal continued to blur. Their stolen glances and lingering touches became more frequent, each one igniting a spark that was becoming impossible to ignore. But Lexi was determined to prove herself, to show that she was more than just Beckett's assistant or his potential lover.

Rachel, ever observant, noticed the growing closeness between them. "Be careful, Lexi," she advised one day. "Mixing work and romance can get messy."

"I know," Lexi replied, grateful for Rachel's concern. "I'm trying to keep things professional."

Despite her best efforts, the boundaries kept shifting. One evening, after another long day, Beckett invited Lexi to join him for dinner at an exclusive restaurant. It was a thinly veiled attempt at a date, and Lexi found herself unable to resist.

The restaurant was exquisite, the kind of place where reservations were booked months in advance. They were seated at a private table, the ambiance intimate and luxurious. As they enjoyed their meal, Beckett's charm and charisma were on full display, making it increasingly difficult for Lexi to maintain her professional distance.

"You look stunning tonight," Beckett said, his voice low and sincere.

Lexi blushed, feeling a warmth spread through her. "Thank you. This place is amazing."

"I wanted to do something special," he replied, his eyes never leaving hers.

As the evening progressed, their conversation flowed effortlessly. They laughed, shared stories, and delved deeper into each other's lives. By the time dessert arrived, the connection between them was undeniable.

"Lexi," Beckett began, his tone serious. "I know this is complicated, but I can't deny how I feel about you."

Lexi's heart pounded in her chest. She knew she was treading dangerous waters, but her feelings for Beckett were too strong to ignore. "I feel the same way, Beckett. But we need to be careful."

"I understand," he said, reaching across the table to take her hand. "We'll take things one step at a time."

As they left the restaurant, Beckett insisted on walking her home. The night air was cool, the city alive with its usual energy. They walked in comfortable silence, the unspoken understanding between them growing stronger with each step.

When they reached Lexi's apartment, Beckett hesitated, his eyes searching hers. "Can I come in?"

Lexi bit her lip, torn between her desire and the need to maintain some semblance of boundaries. "Maybe not tonight. But soon."

He nodded, respecting her decision. "Goodnight, Lexi."

"Goodnight, Beckett."

She watched him walk away, a mixture of emotions swirling within her. Their relationship was evolving, the lines becoming increasingly blurred. But one thing was certain: her feelings for Beckett were real, and she was willing to navigate the complexities that came with them.

The next day at the office, things felt different. There was an unspoken tension, a heightened awareness of each other. Beckett's touches lingered a bit longer, his glances more intense. Lexi found it harder to concentrate, her mind constantly drifting to the night before. Rachel noticed the change, her eyes narrowing slightly as she watched them interact. "You two seem close," she remarked during a coffee break. Lexi hesitated, unsure of how much to reveal. "We've been spending a lot of time together. It's hard not to get close."

Rachel nodded, her expression thoughtful. "Just be careful, Lexi. Mixing work and romance can be tricky."

"I know," Lexi replied, appreciating Rachel's concern. "But I think it's worth it."

The weeks continued to pass in a blur of work and stolen moments. Lexi and Beckett's relationship deepened, the boundaries between their professional and personal lives becoming increasingly blurred. They navigated the complexities with care, aware of the risks but unwilling to deny their feelings.

One evening, as they worked late on a new project, Beckett leaned in close, his breath warm against her ear. "I can't stop thinking about you, Lexi."

Her heart raced, the familiar mix of desire and caution flooding her senses. "Me neither."

He cupped her face in his hands, his eyes searching hers. "What are we doing, Lexi?"

She smiled a hint of sadness in her eyes. "Navigating the chaos. Together."

Beckett's kiss was tender, filled with unspoken promises. At that moment, Lexi knew that no matter the challenges they faced, they would find a way to

make it work. Their love was worth fighting for, worth navigating the blurred lines and complexities of their world.

The following days were a testament to their growing bond. They worked seamlessly together, their professional synergy translating into their personal lives. Beckett's support gave Lexi the confidence to tackle even the most daunting tasks, while her presence grounded him, providing a sense of stability he hadn't realized he needed.

One afternoon, as they prepared for an important presentation, Beckett turned to her, a serious expression on his face. "Lexi, I need to ask you something."

She looked up from her notes, her heart skipping a beat. "What is it?"

He took a deep breath, his eyes intense. "Do you see a future for us? Beyond just this?"

Lexi's breath caught in her throat. She had been grappling with the same question, her feelings for Beckett growing stronger each day. "I do, Beckett. But it's not going to be easy". "I know," he replied, his voice

filled with determination. "But I'm willing to fight for us. If you are."

She smiled, a sense of clarity washing over her. "I am. Let's navigate this together."

As they stood there, facing the challenges ahead, Lexi felt a sense of hope. Their journey was far from over, but with Beckett by her side, she was ready to face whatever came their way.

CHAPTER TEN

SECRETS AND LIES

Lexi had always known that Beckett's world was filled with shadows. Despite the charm, wealth, and influence, she sensed there were parts of him he kept hidden. But what she discovered that fateful afternoon was beyond anything she had imagined.

It started as a normal day at Blackwood Tower. Lexi was handling Beckett's schedule, coordinating meetings, and ensuring everything ran smoothly. Beckett was out for a lunch meeting, giving Lexi a rare moment of quiet in his office. She took the opportunity to organize some files, wanting to prove herself indispensable.

As she was sorting through the papers on Beckett's desk, her hand brushed against something odd—a small button beneath the desk. Curiosity piqued, Lexi pressed it, hearing a soft click. A hidden panel slid open, revealing a small safe embedded in the wall.

Lexi's heart raced. What could Beckett possibly need to hide so securely? She knew she shouldn't invade his

privacy, but an inexplicable urge pushed her forward. She found a keypad and, after a moment of hesitation, decided to try the combination she'd seen him use for other locks: 0621, his late mother's birthday. The safe clicked open.

Inside were several folders, thick with documents, and a flash drive. Lexi took out one of the folders, her hands trembling slightly. She opened it to find a series of financial statements, contracts, and a few photographs. The more she read, the more her blood ran cold. There were names she recognized—powerful people, government officials, and mentions of deals that were far from legal.

Just then, she heard the door open. Lexi's heart jumped to her throat as she quickly shoved the documents back into the safe and closed it, sliding the panel shut just as Beckett walked in.

"Hey, you're still here," he said with a warm smile, oblivious to her panic. "I thought you might have left for lunch."

Lexi forced a smile, her heart pounding. "I just wanted to finish organizing these files."

Beckett walked over, placing a hand on her shoulder. His touch was reassuring, but now it felt different, almost heavy with the secrets she'd just uncovered. "You're amazing, you know that? I don't know what I'd do without you."

"Thanks," she replied, trying to keep her voice steady. "I'm just trying to be helpful."

As Beckett turned to his desk, Lexi's mind raced. She needed to know more, but how could she confront him without revealing she'd been snooping? The rest of the afternoon passed in a blur, her thoughts consumed by what she'd found.

That evening, as they walked out of the building together, Beckett noticed her silence. "Is everything okay, Lexi? You seem a bit distant."

Lexi forced another smile. "Just tired, I guess. It's been a long day."

They parted ways, but Lexi couldn't shake the feeling of unease. At home, she plugged in the flash drive she had discreetly taken from the safe, hoping to find answers. The drive contained more documents, emails, and encrypted files. As she scrolled through the

information, a pattern began to emerge—one that painted a much darker picture of Beckett's empire.

Beckett wasn't just a savvy businessman; he was deeply entangled in a web of corruption, using his influence to manipulate markets and people alike. Lexi's heart sank. The man she was falling for had a side she never knew, a side that threatened to overshadow everything she admired about him.

The next morning, Lexi arrived at Blackwood Tower with a heavy heart. She had to confront Beckett, but how? As she entered his office, she took a deep breath, steeling herself for the conversation ahead.

"Beckett, can we talk?" she asked, her voice trembling slightly.

Beckett looked up from his desk, concern etched on his face. "Of course. What's on your mind?"

Lexi took a seat opposite him, meeting his gaze. "I found something yesterday. In your safe."

Beckett's expression shifted a flicker of something unreadable in his eyes. "What exactly did you find?"

"Documents. About your business dealings. Some of them... they're not legal, Beckett. What's going on?"

For a moment, silence hung heavy between them. Beckett leaned back in his chair, running a hand through his hair. "Lexi, I didn't want you to find out like this."

"Find out what?" Lexi pressed, her voice rising. "That you're involved in illegal activities? That your empire is built on corruption?"

Beckett sighed, his gaze dropping to the floor. "It's complicated, Lexi. There are things you don't understand."

"Then help me understand," she pleaded. "I deserve to know the truth."

He looked at her, his eyes filled with a mixture of guilt and sorrow. "It's true that I've made some questionable decisions. In this world, power and influence come at a price. I've done things I'm not proud of to protect my company and my people."

Lexi's heart ached at the pain in his voice. "But why? You're so talented, Beckett. You didn't need to resort to this."

"It's not that simple," he replied, his tone weary. "When you reach a certain level, the lines between right and wrong start to blur. I've tried to do what's best, but sometimes the choices are impossible."

Lexi felt tears sting her eyes. She had fallen for the man she thought Beckett was, but now she faced the harsh reality of his secrets. "What does this mean for us?"

Beckett stood, crossing the room to kneel beside her chair. "I care about you, Lexi. More than I've cared about anyone in a long time. I want to be honest with you, to let you in. But you have to understand, that my world is dangerous. If you're with me, you could get hurt."

Lexi reached out, her hand trembling as she cupped his face. "I can handle it, Beckett. I just need to know that we're in this together."

He covered her hand with his, his eyes searching hers. "We are. But I need you to promise me something. If things ever get too dangerous, you'll walk away. I couldn't live with myself if something happened to you because of me."

Lexi nodded, her resolve strengthening. "I promise. But I'm not going anywhere right now. We'll figure this out together."

Beckett pulled her into his arms, holding her tightly. "Thank you, Lexi. I don't deserve you, but I'm grateful you're here."

Over the next few days, the dynamic between Lexi and Beckett shifted. They worked closely, their connection deepening even as they navigated the murky waters of Beckett's business. Lexi's resolve to understand and support him only grew stronger.

One evening, as they were working late, Lexi glanced at Beckett, a thought nagging at her. "Beckett, who else knows about these documents?"

He sighed, running a hand through his hair. "A few trusted associates. And now, you."

Lexi nodded, her mind racing. "We need to be careful. If someone else finds out…"

"I know," Beckett interrupted, his expression serious. "That's why I need you to stay vigilant. Some people would do anything to bring me down."

As the days turned into weeks, Lexi found herself caught in a whirlwind of emotions. She was falling deeper for Beckett, but the weight of his secrets hung heavily over them. Their stolen moments of intimacy

were bittersweet, tainted by the knowledge of what lay beneath the surface.

One night, as they lay together in Beckett's penthouse, Lexi couldn't help but voice her fears. "What if this doesn't work, Beckett? What if your past catches up to us?"

He tightened his arms around her, his voice a soothing murmur in the darkness. "We'll face it together, Lexi. I promise you, I'll do everything in my power to keep you safe."

Lexi wanted to believe him, but the doubts lingered. The more she uncovered about Beckett's world, the more she realized how precarious their situation was. But she also knew she couldn't walk away. Her feelings for Beckett were too strong, and she was determined to stand by him, no matter the cost.

Their relationship continued to evolve, each day bringing new challenges and deeper connections. Beckett opened up to Lexi more than he ever had to anyone, sharing his fears, his regrets, and his assurance for the future. Lexi, in turn, found herself falling more in love with him, despite the shadows that loomed over them.

One afternoon, as they were working on a particularly complex deal, Beckett turned to Lexi, his expression thoughtful. "I want to show you something."

Curiosity piqued, Lexi followed him to a hidden alcove in his office. Beckett pressed another concealed button, revealing a second safe. This one, however, contained something entirely different: a collection of personal mementos, photographs, and letters.

"These are the things that matter most to me," Beckett explained, his voice soft. "The people and moments that shaped who I am."

Lexi carefully picked up a photograph of a young Beckett with his parents, their faces beaming with pride. "Your family?"

Beckett nodded, a wistful smile on his lips. "They were everything to me. Losing them was the hardest thing I've ever faced."

Lexi felt a pang of sympathy, her heart aching for the boy who had lost so much. "I'm so sorry, Beckett. I can't imagine how difficult that must have been."

"It was," he admitted, his gaze distant. "But it also made me who I am today. Stronger, more determined. And it taught me the importance of protecting what matters most."

As they looked through the mementos, Lexi felt a deeper connection to Beckett. He wasn't just a powerful billionaire; he was a man shaped by loss, love, and resilience. And despite the darkness of his business dealings, she saw the goodness in him, the desire to make a difference in the world.

That night, as they sat together on the balcony of Beckett's penthouse, Lexi took his hand in hers. "We'll get through this, Beckett. Together. I believe in us."

Beckett turned to her, his eyes filled with emotion. "Thank you, Lexi. Your faith in me means more than you know."

Their kiss was tender, a promise of love and support. As the city lights twinkled below them, Lexi felt a renewed sense of desire. The road ahead was uncertain, but with Beckett by her side, she was ready to face whatever challenges came their way.

CHAPTER ELEVEN

THE SHADOWS CLOSE IN

A note slipped silently under Lexi's apartment door it's like a sudden whisper in a darkened room, unsettling and dangerous. It was an ordinary piece of paper, but the message it carried was anything but mundane. Stop digging or you'll regret it. The uneven script was a glaring reminder that Lexi's quest for truth had not gone unnoticed—and that it had stirred something far more sinister than she had anticipated.

Her heart pounded as she unfolded the note, the scrawled warning striking a chord deep within her. Just hours earlier, she had been engrossed in the latest set of documents, piecing together the disturbing patterns of Beckett's empire. She had found financial discrepancies that pointed to a shadowy network of influence, one that reached into the darkest corners of the city's elite. The revelation had been both thrilling and terrifying. The thrill of uncovering the truth was now overshadowed by a palpable fear of retribution.

As Lexi replayed the events of the day in her mind, her thoughts raced through the implications of the note. The threats were no longer abstract warnings—they were a confrontation. Someone wanted her to stop, and they were willing to resort to intimidation to make sure she did.

Her resolve, however, was not easily shaken. Lexi had always prided herself on her determination, and the threat only fueled her determination to uncover the truth. But the fear was real, and it was creeping into every corner of her life, making even the familiar streets of Manhattan feel hostile and unwelcoming.

That evening, the weight of the note's message drove her to Beckett's penthouse, her nerves on edge as she walked through the opulent corridors of Blackwood Tower. The familiar luxury that once felt comforting now seemed like a gilded cage, hiding dangers she had only begun to understand.

Beckett greeted her with a concerned look, his expression shifting as he took in her pale face and trembling hands. "Lexi, what's wrong?" His voice was a soothing balm against her rising panic.

She handed him the note, her voice barely more than a whisper. "This was under my door."

Beckett's eyes scanned the message, his expression darkening as he read the threat. "I was afraid this might happen," he said, his voice tight with concern. "You've been getting too close to the truth."

Lexi met his gaze, her eyes filled with both fear and determination. "I can't stop now. There's too much at stake."

Beckett's protective instincts flared. "We'll figure this out," he said firmly, wrapping his arms around her in a reassuring embrace. "But you need to be careful. These people don't play games."

The next few days were a blur of heightened tension and constant vigilance. Beckett had increased security around Lexi, but the sense of being watched never left her. Every rustle of leaves, every shadow that moved, made her heart race with apprehension. The threats had become more than just words—they were a constant, suffocating presence in her life.

One evening, as she walked through Central Park, a familiar chill ran down her spine. Her phone buzzed with a new message from an unknown number: Stay away from Beckett Blackwood. The text was a clear and chilling command, the kind of message that could only be meant to instill fear.

Lexi's instincts screamed at her to run, but she forced herself to remain calm. She quickened her pace, her eyes darting around the park for any sign of danger. The peaceful surroundings now felt menacing, each passerby a potential threat. She reached her apartment, locked the door behind her, and immediately called Beckett.

"Lexi, are you okay?" Beckett's voice was filled with concern as he answered on the first ring.

"I got another message," she said, her voice trembling. "They're telling me to stay away from you."

There was a brief silence on the other end of the line, heavy with unspoken fears. "I'm coming over," Beckett said, his tone resolute. "We need to talk."

When Beckett arrived, his presence was a much-needed anchor. He held her tightly, offering comfort and strength as they faced the harsh reality of their situation. "We need to find out who's behind this," he said, his voice steady. "I won't let anyone hurt you."

The threat was now an undeniable part of their reality, and Lexi's determination to uncover the truth grew stronger. The documents she had uncovered hinted at a vast network of corruption, but the true puppet masters remained elusive. With Beckett's support, Lexi continued her investigation, determined to piece together the puzzle despite the ever-present danger.

One late night at Blackwood Tower, as Lexi pored over more files, she stumbled upon an encrypted email that seemed out of place. Her fingers worked deftly, deciphering the code as her eyes widened with each revealing line. The message detailed plans for a hostile takeover, orchestrated by someone close to Beckett—someone she had trusted.

Her heart raced as she realized the magnitude of the betrayal. She rushed to Beckett's office, her breath coming in sharp gasps. "Beckett, I found something," she said urgently.

Beckett looked up from his desk, surprise etched on his face. "What is it?"

Lexi handed him the decrypted email, her hands shaking. Beckett's expression shifted from confusion to shock and anger as he read the message. "This is from

Rachel," he said, his voice tight with disbelief. "She's been working against me."

The revelation was a heavy blow. Rachel, Beckett's trusted assistant, had been a double agent all along. The sense of betrayal was palpable, and the realization of the depth of the deception left them both reeling.

The confrontation with Rachel was intense. Beckett and Lexi cornered her in his office, the air thick with tension and accusation. Rachel's initial shock quickly turned into defiance as she faced Beckett's anger.

"Why, Rachel?" Beckett's voice was strained with hurt and fury. "Why betray me?"

Rachel's eyes were cold, her voice steady. "You've built your empire on lies and deceit. I'm just doing what's necessary to bring you down."

Lexi stepped forward, her voice firm. "And you thought threatening me would help your cause?"

Rachel's sneer was a bitter reminder of the high stakes they faced. "You were getting too close. I couldn't risk you uncovering everything."

With Rachel exposed, Beckett's security team took swift action. She was escorted out of the building, her fate now in the hands of the authorities. But Lexi and Beckett knew that Rachel was just one piece of a much larger puzzle.

That night, as they sat together in Beckett's penthouse, the weight of the day's events hung heavily between them. Lexi leaned against Beckett, seeking solace in his presence. "We've only scratched the surface," she said quietly. "There's still so much we don't know."

CHAPTER TWELVE

THE MASK SLIPS

Lexi sat on the plush leather couch in Beckett's penthouse, the dim glow from the cityscape casting long shadows across the room. The air was thick with unspoken tension. She glanced at Beckett, who was pacing back and forth, a rare display of agitation marring his usually calm demeanor.

"Beckett," Lexi began softly, her voice trembling, "what aren't you telling me?"

He stopped, turning to face her. His eyes, usually so enigmatic and composed, now flickered with something darker, something almost desperate. "There are things you don't understand, Lexi. Things I've kept from you to protect you."

Lexi's heart pounded in her chest. "Protect me? Or control me?"

Beckett's expression hardened. "You think I'm controlling you? After everything I've done to keep you safe?"

"You've been manipulating me, Beckett. I've seen the documents and the connections. You've used your influence to orchestrate everything around me," Lexi said, her voice rising with each word. "You even used Rachel to keep tabs on me."

Beckett took a step closer, his presence imposing. "I did what I had to do. To protect my interests. To protect you."

"Protect me from what?" Lexi demanded, standing her ground. "From the truth?"

The silence that followed was suffocating. Beckett's mask was slipping, and the man beneath was someone Lexi barely recognized. His gaze held hers, a mix of frustration and something far more unsettling.

"You don't understand the world I live in, Lexi," Beckett said, his voice low and intense. "The power, the influence—it comes at a cost. There are things I've done, choices I've made... for us."

Lexi felt a shiver run down her spine. "For us? Or for you?"

Beckett's jaw clenched, his control slipping further. "You have no idea what it's like to carry this burden. To have the world at your feet but know that one wrong move can bring it all crashing down."

"Then let me in," Lexi pleaded, her voice softening. "Let me help you carry it."

For a moment, Beckett's facade cracked, revealing the vulnerability underneath. But it was fleeting, replaced quickly by the stern, calculating man she'd come to know.

"I can't," he said, turning away. "It's too dangerous."

Lexi's heart ached. She reached out, her hand gently touching his arm. "Beckett, whatever it is, we can face it together. But you have to trust me."

He pulled away, his expression a mix of anger and pain. "Trust you? When you've been snooping around behind my back?"

Lexi stepped back, stung by his accusation. "I was trying to understand you. To understand why you've been so secretive."

Beckett's eyes softened, but his resolve remained. "There are some things you're better off not knowing."

"Like what?" Lexi pressed. "What are you so afraid of?"

He sighed, running a hand through his hair. "Losing you. Losing everything I've worked so hard to protect."

Lexi's breath caught in her throat. "Beckett, you won't lose me. But I can't live in the dark. I need to know the truth."

The room fell silent again, the weight of their conversation hanging heavy in the air. Beckett looked at her, his eyes searching hers for a long moment. Finally, he spoke, his voice barely above a whisper.

"There are people who would stop at nothing to bring me down. People who have already tried. I've kept you in the dark because the less you know, the safer you are."

Lexi shook her head. "But keeping secrets from me isn't the answer. We need to face this together."

Beckett's shoulders slumped, the fight draining out of him. "You don't know what you're asking."

"Maybe not," Lexi admitted. "But I know that I love you. And I can't stand by while you push me away."

For the first time, Beckett seemed to see her, to understand the depth of her resolve. He took a step forward, closing the distance between them. "You're right. I've been trying to protect you in all the wrong ways."

Lexi's eyes filled with tears. "Then let me in. Let me help you."

Beckett reached out, his hand cupping her cheek. "I'm sorry, Lexi. I've been a fool."

She leaned into his touch, her heart aching for him. "We'll face this together, Beckett. No more secrets."

CHAPTER THIRTEEN

BENEATH THE SURFACE

The soft hum of Lexi's laptop was the only sound breaking the silence in her Brooklyn Heights apartment. She was sifting through old emails and documents, trying to organize her thoughts and sort out the chaos in her mind. Her desk was cluttered with paper stacks, coffee cups, and an assortment of office supplies—a familiar sight for anyone who knew her work habits.

But amidst the disorder, a new file caught her eye. It had arrived that morning through an encrypted email, an unexpected delivery she had initially dismissed as spam. The subject line read: "Confidential File—Action Required."

Curiosity got the better of her, and she opened it. The file contained a series of documents and scans that detailed intricate financial transactions and contracts. As Lexi scanned through the data, her heart raced. She recognized the names and companies mentioned in the documents, including several high-profile entities connected to Beckett's empire.

The file was meticulously organized, with sections highlighting various deals and financial maneuvers. One document stood out: a contract tied to a controversial business deal from years ago. It was filled with technical jargon and legalese, but the crux was clear—a significant amount of money had been involved, and it seemed that the deal had negatively impacted numerous people.

Lexi's hands shook as she dug deeper. The documents hinted at shady practices and questionable decisions, all pointing back to Beckett's involvement. She clicked through several pages, each one revealing more about a past she had only heard whispers of. The file made it clear: Beckett's wealth was not just a product of his business acumen but also of decisions that had led to financial devastation for others.

With every click, Lexi's anxiety grew. This wasn't just idle gossip; these were concrete records that painted Beckett in a troubling light. The more she read, the more her stomach churned. She felt as though she was intruding on a hidden part of Beckett's world, one he had kept from her for reasons she could only guess.

The documents were sent anonymously, but the implications were too real. Lexi found herself staring at the screen, feeling the weight of the secrets she had uncovered. Her mind raced with questions and doubts. How could Beckett have kept something so significant hidden? And why did someone want her to know about it now?

As the sun dipped below the horizon, casting long shadows in her apartment, Lexi decided she needed to confront Beckett. The gravity of what she had discovered was too much to handle alone. She gathered the documents, putting them in a folder for easy access. Her heart pounded as she prepared to face the man she had come to care for deeply.

The elevator ride up to Blackwood Tower seemed endless. Each floor felt like a mile, each moment stretching out with agonizing slowness. Lexi's thoughts churned—what if Beckett's explanations were as layered and complex as the documents themselves?

Could he truly justify his actions, or was this the end of their burgeoning relationship?

When Lexi stepped into Beckett's penthouse, the grandeur of the space did nothing to ease her anxiety. The apartment was an opulent display of wealth, with its sleek furniture, floor-to-ceiling windows, and tasteful art pieces. Yet, as she walked toward Beckett's office, all she could focus on was the confrontation ahead.

Beckett was at his desk, the warm glow of the desk lamp illuminating his face. He looked up as Lexi entered, his expression shifting from surprise to concern. "Lexi, what a surprise. Is everything all right?"

Lexi took a deep breath, forcing herself to stay calm. "Beckett, we need to talk. I found something today that I need to discuss with you."

Beckett's brow furrowed, his smile fading. "What's wrong?"

Lexi approached the desk, placing the folder in front of him. "I received an anonymous file this morning. It contains documents about a business deal you were involved in. The deal that caused a lot of harm to people."

Beckett's expression grew serious as he opened the folder and glanced at the documents inside. His face paled slightly, and he looked up at Lexi, a mixture of apprehension and regret in his eyes. "Lexi, I can explain."

Lexi's voice trembled as she spoke. "Explain? How do you explain this? How do you justify keeping something like this from me?"

Beckett's gaze dropped to the documents, his eyes scanning the pages. "It's not as simple as it looks. That deal was a part of a larger strategy. At the time, I was pressured into making those decisions, and I didn't see the full consequences. When I realized the impact, it was too late."

Lexi shook her head, her frustration palpable. "You should have told me. I needed to know about this before I found it myself. Now, I'm left to question everything I thought I knew about you."

Beckett stood up, his voice pleading. "Lexi, I've tried to make amends in whatever way I could. I didn't want to burden you with my past, but I see now that hiding it only made things worse. I'm not that man anymore."

Lexi's heart ached as she looked at him. "But how can I trust that you've changed? How can I believe that the man I've come to care for is genuine when there's so much deception?"

Beckett's shoulders slumped, and he walked to the window, staring out at the city below. "I understand if you're angry. I'm willing to do whatever it takes to prove myself to you. I want to be honest with you now, even if it's too late."

Lexi's eyes blazed with anger as she faced Beckett. "Just leave me alone, Beckett. Let me be!" she spat, her voice trembling with rage.

Beckett took a step closer, his hands reaching out to calm her down. "Lexi, please—"

But Lexi was having none of it. "Do not touch me!" she warned, her voice rising. "I said get out!"

Beckett's face fell, but he reluctantly turned and walked away, the weight of his regret evident in his slow, heavy footsteps.

CHAPTER FOURTEEN

INTO THE ABYSS

The city outside Beckett's penthouse window was cloaked in twilight, its usual vibrancy muted by the encroaching darkness. The lights of Manhattan sparkled like scattered diamonds against a black velvet backdrop, but the beauty of the view was lost on Lexi.

Beckett stood outside the room door, his knuckles rapping out a steady rhythm as he pleaded for forgiveness. "Lexi, please open up. I'm sorry. I was wrong. Can we talk?"

Minutes ticked by, but Beckett didn't give up. He continued to knock and apologize, his voice growing hoarse from the effort. Finally, the door creaked open, and Lexi stood before him, her eyes red-rimmed from crying. Beckett's heart sank, but he pressed on, his voice filled with contrition.

"Lexi, please... I'm so sorry. Can we talk?" Lexi's gaze searched his face, her expression unreadable. Beckett held his breath, hoping against hope that she would listen, that she would forgive him.

As they entered the guest room, Beckett began to explain. "Lexi, I know I've hurt you. I know I've lied to you. But it was all because I wanted to protect you."

Lexi's eyes narrowed, her voice barely above a whisper. "Protect me from what?"

Beckett hesitated, unsure of how much to reveal. But he knew he had to be honest if he wanted to regain Lexi's trust. "From the truth about my past, about the secrets I've kept. I was afraid that if you knew, you'd leave me."

Lexi's expression softened slightly, her gaze searching Beckett's face for any sign of insincerity. Beckett held his breath, hoping that she would see the truth in his eyes.

"I was wrong to deceive you," Beckett continued, his voice cracking with emotion. "I was wrong to manipulate you. But everything I did, it was because I love you."

Lexi's voice trembled as she spoke. "Talk? About how everything I thought I knew about you is a lie?"

Beckett took a step toward her, his hands raised in a gesture of peace. "It's not like that. I never wanted to hurt you."

But Lexi was beyond consolation. "You've been manipulating me from the start. Using your power, your influence—it's all been a game to you."

Beckett's expression twisted with pain. "No, Lexi. I did what I had to do to protect you."

"Protect me?" she scoffed, the anger in her voice rising. "Or control me?"

Beckett sighed, running a hand through his hair. "I can't deny that I've made mistakes. But everything I've done, it was because I love you."

Lexi felt her resolve waver. Love—it was the word that had kept her tethered to Beckett despite everything. But now, that love felt tainted, overshadowed by the darkness she had uncovered. "Love shouldn't feel like this," she whispered. "It shouldn't feel like a trap."

Beckett stepped closer, his gaze pleading. "Give me a chance to explain. To make things right."

She shook her head, tears streaming down her cheeks. "I don't know if I can trust you anymore."

The days that followed were a blur of tension and heartache. Lexi found herself trapped in a whirlwind of emotions, torn between her feelings for Beckett and the undeniable truth of his manipulations. She spent hours pouring over the uncovered documents, hoping to find some redeeming evidence to absolve Beckett of his wrongdoings. But the more she looked, the clearer it became—Beckett's empire was built on foundations of deceit and corruption.

One evening, Lexi found herself alone in Beckett's penthouse. The silence was suffocating, the shadows creeping in from every corner. She wandered through the luxurious rooms, her mind a tumultuous sea of thoughts and memories. Every piece of art, every piece of furniture seemed to mock her, reminding her of the life she had been drawn into—a life that now felt like a gilded cage.

Her eyes fell on Beckett's office door, the room that had become a symbol of his secrets. Taking a deep breath, she pushed the door open and stepped inside. The room was dark, the only light coming from the city skyline outside the large windows. She moved to Beckett's desk, her fingers tracing the polished wood surface as she sat down in his chair.

Lexi opened the drawer that held the key to the hidden safe she had discovered weeks ago. She had found more documents there, each one more damning than the last. A sense of dread washed over her as she pulled out the files. She knew what she needed to do, but the thought of confronting Beckett again filled her with fear.

A sudden noise broke the silence, startling her. She turned to see Beckett standing in the doorway, his expression a mix of surprise and concern. "What are you doing in here?" he asked, his voice tense.

Lexi met his gaze, her heart pounding. "I needed to see for myself," she said, holding up the documents. "I needed to understand."

Beckett's face hardened. "And what did you find?"

"More lies," she replied, her voice trembling. "More secrets. Beckett, I can't live like this. I can't live in a world where I don't know if I can trust the man I love."

He took a step toward her, his eyes filled with desperation. "Lexi, please. Let me explain."

She stood up, her resolve firm. "No more explanations. No more lies. I need to get out of here. I need to find a way to survive without you."

The decision to leave Beckett was the hardest thing Lexi had ever done. But the need for self-preservation outweighed her love for him. She packed her things quickly, her movements driven by a sense of urgency. She didn't know where she would go or what she would do, but she knew she had to get away from the suffocating grip of Beckett's world.

As she was about to leave, Beckett appeared in the doorway, blocking her path. "Where are you going?" he asked, his voice a mix of anger and desperation.

Lexi took a deep breath, steeling herself. "I need to go. I need to find my way."

"You're making a mistake," Beckett said, his eyes flashing with a dangerous intensity. "You won't survive without me."

"I'll find a way," she replied, her voice steady. "I have to."

With a final look of determination, Lexi pushed past Beckett and walked out of the penthouse. The elevator ride down felt like an eternity, each floor a step closer to her independence. When the doors finally opened, she stepped out into the bustling streets of Manhattan, the noise and energy of the city a stark contrast to the suffocating silence of Beckett's penthouse.

The days that followed were a test of Lexi's strength and resilience. She found a small apartment on the outskirts of the city, far from the luxury and opulence she had grown accustomed to. It was a modest place, but it was hers, and that was enough.

Lexi threw herself into her work, using her skills and connections to build a new life. She took on freelance projects, helping small businesses with their marketing and events. It was a far cry from the high-profile events she had planned with Beckett, but it was fulfilling in its way.

Despite her efforts to move on, Beckett's presence lingered like a shadow over her life. She would see his name in the news, and hear whispers of his influence in the business world. But she resisted the urge to reach out, knowing that she needed to stand on her own.

One evening, as she was working late, there was a knock on her door. Lexi's heart raced as she approached, her mind racing with possibilities. When she opened the door, she was shocked to see Beckett standing there, his expression weary and desperate.

"Lexi," he said, his voice soft. "I need to talk to you."

She hesitated, torn between the love she still felt for him and the need to protect herself. "What do you want, Beckett?"

"I've made mistakes," he admitted, his eyes filled with regret. "But I can't let you go. I need you."

Lexi's heart ached at his words, but she knew she couldn't go back to the way things were. "You need to let me go," she said, her voice firm. "I can't be with you if I can't trust you."

Beckett took a step closer, his eyes pleading. "Give me a chance to make things right. Please."

Lexi's resolve wavered, but she forced herself to stay strong. "I need time," she said. "Time to figure out who I am without you."

The weeks that followed were a difficult period of self-discovery for Lexi. She threw herself into her work, finding solace in the tasks that filled her days. She reconnected with old friends, seeking support and guidance as she navigated the complexities of her new life.

One evening, as she sat in her apartment, Lexi received a package in the mail. Inside was a letter from Beckett, along with a stack of documents. The letter was filled with heartfelt apologies and explanations, and the documents detailed his efforts to dismantle the corrupt network he had been a part of.

Lexi's heart ached as she read Beckett's words, his sincerity, and remorse evident in every line. She knew he was trying to make amends, to prove that he was willing to change. But she also knew that trust couldn't be rebuilt overnight.

The decision to meet with Beckett again was not an easy one. Lexi spent hours weighing the pros and cons, her mind a battleground of conflicting emotions. But in the end, she knew she had to face him, to see if there was any hope for their future.

They met in a small café, far from the grandeur of Beckett's world. The atmosphere was quiet and intimate, a stark contrast to the tension that hung between them.

"Thank you for meeting me," Beckett said, his voice tentative.

Lexi nodded, her heart pounding. "I read your letter."

"I meant every word," he said, his eyes filled with sincerity. "I'm trying to make things right."

"I can see that," Lexi replied, her voice soft. "But trust isn't something that can be easily rebuilt."

"I know," Beckett said, his expression pained. "But I'm willing to do whatever it takes. I love you, Lexi. And I don't want to lose you."

Lexi's heart ached at his words, but she knew she had to protect herself. "I need time, Beckett. Time to see if we can rebuild what we had."

Beckett nodded, his eyes filled with determination. "I'll wait as long as it takes."

The path to recovery was not an easy one. Lexi and Beckett took things slow, rebuilding their relationship one step at a time. There were moments of doubt and fear, but also moments of anticipation and love. They learned to communicate openly and to trust each other in ways they hadn't before.

As the months passed, Lexi began to see the changes in Beckett. He was more open, more vulnerable. He had dismantled the corrupt network, taking responsibility for his actions and working to make amends.

Their love, once tainted by secrets and lies, began to grow stronger, rooted in honesty and trust. Lexi knew that the road ahead would not be easy, but she was willing to take the journey with Beckett, knowing that their love was worth fighting for.

Lexi's journey into the abyss has been a test of her strength and resilience. She has faced the darkness and emerged stronger, finding the courage to begin again.

CHAPTER FIFTEEN

THE FALLOUT

The morning light filtered through the thin curtains of Lexi's modest apartment, casting a gentle glow over the room. The soft hum of Manhattan waking up outside provided a stark contrast to the chaos that had become her life. Sitting at her small kitchen table, Lexi cradled a cup of coffee in her hands, the warmth seeping through the ceramic into her fingertips. It was a rare moment of peace, but even this tranquility was shadowed by the memories of Beckett and the life she had left behind.

This wasn't just any ordinary day. This was the beginning of Lexi's journey to reclaim her life. The path she had chosen was riddled with uncertainty, but she was determined to walk it, no matter how difficult it might be.

The day began like many others, with Lexi trying to piece together the fragments of her broken world. The scars of her past were still raw, but each day brought new strength. Her first step was reaching out to someone she never thought she'd rely on—Rachel, Beckett's former assistant. Lexi knew Rachel had been instrumental in the chaos, but she also believed in second chances and the possibility of redemption.

Lexi dialed Rachel's number with a sense of trepidation, unsure of how the conversation would unfold. The phone rang a few times before Rachel answered, her voice cautious.

"Hello?"

"Rachel, it's Lexi," she said, her voice steady despite her nerves. "I think we need to talk."

There was a pause on the other end of the line, followed by a sigh. "Lexi, I didn't expect to hear from you. What's going on?"

"I need your help," Lexi admitted. "I know we have a complicated history, but I think you understand Beckett's world better than anyone. I need to figure out how to move forward."

Rachel hesitated, but then her tone softened. "Okay, let's meet. There's a café on 45th Street. Can you be there in an hour?"

"Yes, I'll be there," Lexi agreed, feeling a mix of relief and anxiety.

The café was a cozy, nondescript place tucked away from the bustling streets. Lexi arrived early, choosing a table near the back where they could talk without interruption. She ordered a coffee and waited, her mind racing with questions and doubts.

Rachel walked in a few minutes later, her expression a mix of curiosity and wariness. She spotted Lexi and made her way over, sitting down across from her.

"Thank you for meeting me," Lexi began, taking a deep breath. "I know we didn't part on the best terms."

Rachel nodded, her eyes scanning Lexi's face. "I didn't expect to hear from you, but I understand why you reached out. What do you need to know?"

Lexi leaned forward, her voice earnest. "I need to understand the full extent of Beckett's influence. Even now, I feel like he's still a part of my life, controlling things from the shadows. How do I move past that?"

Rachel sighed, stirring her tea absently. "Beckett's reach is vast, Lexi. He has connections in every sector, and his influence isn't easily shaken. But you're strong, and you've already taken the first step by leaving him. The next step is reclaiming your identity, piece by piece."

As they talked, Lexi felt a weight lift off her shoulders. Rachel provided insights into Beckett's operations, giving Lexi a clearer picture of the challenges ahead. It wasn't going to be easy, but at least she knew what she was up against.

Their conversation was interrupted by the arrival of Detective James, a tall, imposing figure with a stern expression. Lexi had contacted him after her escape, hoping he could help her navigate the legal complexities of her situation.

"Lexi," he greeted, nodding to Rachel. "I didn't expect to find you here."

"Detective James," Lexi replied, standing to shake his hand. "Thank you for coming. Rachel and I were just discussing how to move forward."

James sat down, his gaze sharp and focused. "You've made the right decision, reaching out to Rachel. Her insights are invaluable. But we need to be careful. Beckett won't take kindly to your defiance."

Lexi nodded, her resolve strengthening. "I understand. But I'm not going to let fear dictate my life anymore. I need to reclaim my independence, and I'll do whatever it takes."

James leaned back, his expression thoughtful. "We'll need to build a solid case against Beckett. His influence is extensive, but it's not unbreakable. With Rachel's help, we can gather the evidence we need."

The days that followed were a whirlwind of activity. Lexi worked closely with Rachel and Detective James, piecing together the puzzle of Beckett's operations. Each revelation brought a mix of shock and determination, fueling her resolve to break free from his shadow.

Lexi spent hours going through documents, making phone calls, and meeting with key individuals who could provide crucial information. It was exhausting work, but it was also empowering. For the first time in a long while, she felt like she had control over her life.

One evening, as Lexi was pouring over yet another stack of files, Rachel walked in with a weary smile. "You're making incredible progress, Lexi. I'm impressed."

Lexi looked up, her eyes tired but determined. "Thank you, Rachel. I couldn't have done this without your help."

Rachel sat down across from her, her expression serious. "I need to tell you something, Lexi. Beckett is planning something big. I don't know all the details, but I've heard whispers. We need to be prepared."

Lexi's heart raced, the familiar fear threatening to overwhelm her. But she pushed it aside, focusing on the task at hand. "What can we do?"

"We need to stay ahead of him," Rachel replied. "Keep gathering evidence, and be ready to act when the time comes."

The tension in the air was palpable as Lexi, Rachel, and Detective James continued their work. They knew that every step they took brought them closer to a confrontation with Beckett, but there was no turning back.

Lexi found solace in the support of her friends. Rachel's knowledge and insight were invaluable, and Detective James's unwavering determination provided a sense of security. Together, they formed a formidable team, united by a common goal.

One night, as they were working late, Detective James received a call. His expression grew serious as he listened, and when he hung up, he turned to Lexi and Rachel.

"We've got a lead," he said, his voice tense. "Beckett's planning a major move tomorrow. We need to act fast."

Lexi felt a surge of adrenaline, her mind racing with possibilities. "What do we need to do?"

James outlined their plan, his tone confident. "We'll gather the evidence we need and confront Beckett. It's risky, but it's our best chance to take him down."

The next day, Lexi, Rachel, and Detective James gathered in the precinct, pouring over the evidence they had collected. But as they scrutinized deeper, they began to realize that their case wasn't as airtight as they thought.

"I don't know, guys," Detective James said, rubbing his temples. "We're missing a crucial piece of evidence. Without it, our case is circumstantial at best."

Lexi frowned, her mind racing. "But what about the documents we found? The ones that showed Beckett's involvement in the scandal?"

Rachel shook her head. "Those documents can be explained away. Beckett's lawyers will tear them apart."

The trio sat in silence, the weight of their doubts settling in. They had been so sure they had enough evidence to bring Beckett down, but now they weren't so sure.

Days passed, and they continued to gather evidence, but it was like trying to grasp smoke - the more they thought they had, the more it slipped through their fingers.

Finally, they decided to pay a visit to Beckett's penthouse, hoping to find something, anything, that would solidify their case. As they entered the penthouse, they were met with an eerie silence. Beckett was nowhere to be found, but his presence seemed to linger in the air.

Lexi felt a shiver run down her spine as she realized that they might have been wrong about Beckett all along. Maybe he wasn't the mastermind they thought he was. Maybe he was just a pawn in a much larger game.

The trio searched the penthouse but found nothing concrete. No incriminating evidence. Just a whole lot of nothing.

As they left the penthouse, Lexi couldn't shake off the feeling that they had been outsmarted. That Beckett was still one step ahead of them.

In the days that followed, Lexi worked to start anew. The process was slow, but each step brought her closer to the life she wanted. She found solace in her work, in the support of her friends, and in the knowledge that she had taken control of her destiny.

Rachel became a trusted ally, their bond strengthened by the trials they had faced together. Detective James continued to provide support, his unwavering determination a constant source of strength.

As Lexi sat in her apartment one evening, reflecting on the journey she had taken, she felt a sense of peace. The path had been difficult, but she had emerged stronger, and more resilient. She knew that the future would bring its challenges, but she was ready to face them head-on.

As the city lights twinkled outside Lexi's window, she couldn't help but feel a pang of sadness. Despite everything, there was a part of her that mourned the loss of the love she once believed in. The memories of Beckett, the moments of genuine connection amidst the deceit, lingered like ghosts.

And in that quiet moment, Lexi allowed herself to grieve. For the love that could have been, for the dreams that were shattered. She knew she had to move forward, but it was okay to feel the weight of what she had lost. Sometimes, the most courageous act is to embrace the pain, to let it wash over you, and then, to rise again with renewed strength.

Lexi's journey was far from over, and as she wiped away a tear, she made a silent promise to herself. She would not let the past define her. She would heal, she would grow, and she would find love again—one that was true and pure, untainted by the shadows of the past.

Amid our struggles, there is always hope. And as Lexi drifted off to sleep, a newfound sense of hope bloomed within her heart, guiding her toward a brighter tomorrow.

CHAPTER SIXTEEN

THE RECKONING

The early morning fog clung to the towering buildings of Manhattan, shrouding the city in a misty veil. It was a day that promised to be memorable, the kind that would etch itself into the history of Lexi's life. The tension in the air was palpable, a prelude to the storm that was about to break. Today, everything would come to a head.

This wasn't just any ordinary day. This was the day Lexi had been preparing for, the day she would confront Beckett one last time and ensure he paid for his sins. The stakes were higher than ever, and the weight of justice hung heavy on her shoulders.

Lexi stood at the entrance of Blackwood Tower, the imposing skyscraper that had once seemed so glamorous now felt like a fortress of deceit. She took a deep breath, steeling herself for what lay ahead. She was no longer the same woman who had fallen for Beckett's charms. She was stronger, wiser, and ready to face the darkness head-on.

Detective James was waiting for her just inside the lobby, his expression serious but supportive. "Are you ready for this, Lexi?" he asked, his voice a steady anchor in the storm of emotions swirling inside her.

Lexi nodded, her resolve firm. "I am. It's time Beckett faces the consequences of his actions."

James gave her a reassuring smile. "We've got everything we need. He can't escape this time."

They rode the elevator to the top floor in silence, the hum of the machinery the only sound. Lexi's heart pounded in her chest, each beat a reminder of how far she had come. When the doors opened, they stepped out into the sleek, modern offices of Blackwood Enterprises. The air was thick with anticipation.

Beckett was seated at his desk, his expression unreadable as Lexi and James entered his office. His eyes met Lexi's, and for a moment, she saw a flicker of the man she had once loved. But that moment passed quickly, replaced by the cold, calculating gaze of the man who had betrayed her.

"Lexi," Beckett said, his voice calm but strained. "I wasn't expecting you."

"I'm sure you weren't," Lexi replied, her voice steady. "But we need to talk, Beckett. It's time for the truth to come out."

Detective James stepped forward, placing a stack of documents on Beckett's desk. "Mr. Blackwood, we have enough evidence to charge you with multiple counts of fraud, embezzlement, and conspiracy. It's over."

Beckett's face remained impassive, but Lexi could see the tension in his jaw. "And you think this will bring me down? You have no idea what you're up against."

Lexi took a step closer, her eyes locked on Beckett's. "This isn't just about bringing you down, Beckett. This is about justice. You've hurt so many people, and it's time you faced the consequences."

The confrontation was intense, emotions running high as Beckett tried to defend himself. He argued he threatened, but the evidence was overwhelming. Lexi stood her ground, her resolve unwavering.

"Why, Beckett?" she finally asked, her voice breaking. "Why did you do all of this? Was it worth it?"

For a moment, Beckett's façade cracked, and Lexi saw a glimpse of the man behind the mask. "I did what I had to do," he said quietly. "For power, for control. I thought I could have it all."

"But at what cost?" Lexi pressed. "You've destroyed lives, including mine. Was it worth it?"

Beckett looked away, unable to meet her gaze. "I don't expect you to understand," he said, his voice hollow.

"I don't need to understand," Lexi replied, her voice strong. "I just need to know that you'll face justice."

Detective James stepped forward to restrain Beckett, but Lexi halted him with a raised hand. She needed one last moment with Beckett, a final opportunity to say her piece.

"Beckett," she said softly, her voice filled with a mixture of sorrow and determination. "I loved you once. I believed in you. But you betrayed that trust in the worst way possible. I hope you find a way to make amends, to become a better person. But I can't be a part of that journey."

Beckett's eyes finally met hers, and for a moment, there was a flicker of regret. "Lexi, I'm sorry," he said, his voice barely above a whisper. "For everything."

Lexi nodded, tears brimming in her eyes. "Goodbye, Beckett."

"Mr. Blackwood, you're under arrest," James said, his voice firm. "We have enough evidence against you."

As Detective James led Beckett away, Lexi felt a mixture of relief and sorrow. It was over. The man who had once held her heart was now facing the consequences of his actions, and she was free to move forward.

The days that followed were a blur of legal proceedings and media attention. Lexi found herself thrust into the spotlight, her story capturing the public's imagination. But through it all, she remained focused on her goal: rebuilding her life and finding closure.

Rachel was a constant source of support, and their bond was strengthened by the trials they had faced together. Detective James continued to provide guidance, his unwavering determination a steady anchor in the storm.

One evening, as Lexi sat in her apartment, she received a call from Rachel. "Lexi, I have something for you," Rachel said, her voice excited. "Can you meet me at the café?"

When Lexi arrived at the café, Rachel was already there, a small box in her hands. "What's this?" Lexi asked, curiosity piqued.

Rachel smiled, handing her the box. "It's something I found while going through Beckett's files. I think you should have it."

Lexi opened the box to find a stack of letters, each one addressed to her. She recognized Beckett's handwriting immediately. "What are these?"

"They're letters Beckett wrote to you," Rachel explained. "I think they're his way of trying to make amends."

Lexi's hands trembled as she picked up the first letter, her heart heavy with emotion. She began to read, Beckett's words bringing a mix of pain and closure.

My dearest Lexi,

If you're reading this, it means I've finally faced the consequences of my actions. I know I've hurt you in ways that can never be fully healed, and for that, I am truly sorry. I don't expect forgiveness, but I wish you can find it in your heart to understand why I did what I did.

As you read these letters, know that I love you. In my flawed way, I loved you deeply. But my ambition, my need for control, it overshadowed everything else. I lost sight of what truly mattered.

I hope you can find peace, Lexi. I hope you can move forward and find the happiness you deserve. You are strong, and I have no doubt you will rebuild your life and find love again.

Be happy, Lexi. That's all I ever wanted for you. Yours always,

Beckett

Tears streamed down Lexi's face as she read the letters, each one a window into Beckett's soul. The man she had loved was flawed, deeply so, but there had been moments of genuine love and regret. It was a bittersweet revelation, but it brought a sense of closure.

Rachel reached across the table, squeezing Lexi's hand. "You've come so far, Lexi. I'm proud of you."

Lexi smiled through her tears, grateful for the support of her friend. "Thank you, Rachel. I couldn't have done this without you."

As Lexi walked home that evening, the city lights twinkling around her, she felt a sense of peace she hadn't felt in a long time. The road ahead was still uncertain, but she was ready to face it with strength and resilience.

She knew there would be challenges, moments of doubt, and pain. But she also knew that she had the support of her friends and the strength to overcome anything life threw her way.

And as she looked up at the stars, she made a silent promise to herself: to live her life to the fullest, to embrace each moment with love and courage. The past was behind her, and the future was a blank canvas, waiting to be painted with the colors of her dreams.

As Lexi drifted off to sleep that night, a final tear slipped down her cheek. It wasn't a tear of sorrow, but one of hope and recovery. For in the depths of her heart, she knew that true love was still out there, waiting for her. And she would find it, one day, when the time was right.

So remember this, even in the darkest of times, there is always a glimmer of light. And as Lexi's story continued to unfold, she carried that light within her, guiding her toward a brighter, more beautiful tomorrow.

The next morning, Lexi woke up with a renewed sense of purpose. The sun streamed through her window, casting a warm glow over her apartment. She felt lighter as if a great weight had been lifted from her shoulders. Today was the beginning of a new chapter in her life.

She decided to visit a small park nearby, a place she used to go when she needed to think. The park was quiet, the early morning dew glistening on the grass. Lexi found a bench and sat down, taking in the serene beauty around her.

As she sat there, her mind drifted to Beckett. Despite everything, she couldn't deny that she had loved him deeply. The memories they had shared, both good and bad, would always be a part of her. But she also knew that it was time to let go and move forward.

A soft voice broke her reverie. "Mind if I join you?"

Lexi looked up to see Detective James standing there, his expression gentle. She nodded, gesturing for him to sit. "Of course, James. It's good to see you."

James sat down beside her, his presence comforting. "How are you holding up?"

Lexi sighed, a small smile playing on her lips. "Better. I've had time to reflect and find some closure."

James nodded, his eyes filled with understanding. "I'm glad to hear that, Lexi. You've been through so much, and you deserve to find peace."

They sat in companionable silence for a while, watching as the park slowly came to life with the hustle and bustle of morning activities. Children played, dogs barked, and the sound of laughter filled the air. It was a stark contrast to the turmoil Lexi had faced, a reminder that life goes on.

After a while, James turned to Lexi, his expression serious. "Lexi, I wanted to tell you something. Throughout this whole ordeal, I've been deeply impressed by your strength and resilience. You've handled everything with grace and courage."

Lexi blushed, feeling a warmth spread through her. "Thank you, James. That means a lot coming from you". James hesitated for a moment, then continued. "I've come to care about you, Lexi. More than just a professional relationship. I want you to know that I'm here for you, not just as a detective, but as a friend."

Lexi's heart skipped a beat. She had always admired James, but she had never considered the possibility of something more. She looked into his eyes, seeing the sincerity there. "James, I care about you too. You've been a constant support through all of this, and I'm grateful for your presence in my life."

Their conversation was interrupted by the ringing of Lexi's phone. She glanced at the screen, seeing an unfamiliar number. "Excuse me for a moment," she said, answering the call.

"Hello, is this Lexi?" a woman's voice asked. "Yes, this is Lexi. Who's calling?"

"My name is Dr. Emily Carter. I'm a therapist, and I've been working with some of Beckett's former employees. One of them mentioned your name, and I wanted to reach out to you."

Lexi's heart raced. "What is this about, Dr. Carter?"

"I understand you've been through a lot recently. I wanted to offer my services to you, free of charge.

Sometimes, talking to someone can help with the recovery process."

Lexi was taken aback by the offer. She had never considered therapy, but the idea of talking to someone who could help her navigate her emotions was appealing. "Thank you, Dr. Carter. I appreciate the offer. Can we schedule an appointment?"

"Of course. I'll send you the details. Take care, Lexi."

As Lexi hung up the phone, she felt a sense of relief. Maybe talking to someone would help her heal faster. She turned to James, who was watching her with concern.

"Everything okay?" he asked.

Lexi nodded. "Yes. That was a therapist offering her services. I think I might give it a try."

James smiled, his eyes filled with warmth. "That's a great idea, Lexi. You deserve to heal and find happiness."

Over the next few weeks, Lexi began to see Dr. Carter regularly. The sessions were intense, delving into her past and the trauma she had experienced. But each session brought her closer to understanding herself and finding closure.

One afternoon, after a particularly emotional session, Lexi decided to visit a small bookstore she loved. The smell of old books and the quiet ambiance provided a sense of comfort. As she browsed the shelves, she came across a book that caught her eye.

It was a collection of poetry, filled with words of love, loss, and healing. Lexi picked it up, flipping through the pages. One poem in particular stood out to her:

In the darkest of nights, a glimmer of light, Guides us through the storm, to a future bright.

With strength in our hearts, and hope in our souls, We rise from the ashes and make ourselves whole.

Lexi felt a tear slip down her cheek as she read the words. They resonated with her deeply, a reminder that she was on a journey of restoration and self-discovery.

As she left the bookstore, book in hand, she bumped into someone. "Oh, I'm so sorry," she said, looking up to see a familiar face.

It was Rachel, her eyes wide with surprise. "Lexi! What a coincidence. How are you?"

Lexi smiled, grateful for the unexpected encounter. "I'm doing well, Rachel. Just taking things one day at a time."

Rachel nodded, her expression thoughtful. "I've been thinking about you a lot. You've been through so much, and yet here you are, standing strong."

Lexi felt a surge of gratitude. "Thank you, Rachel. Your support has meant the world to me."

They decided to grab a coffee and catch up. As they sat in the cozy café, the conversation flowed easily. They talked about their lives, their desires, and their dreams. Lexi realized how much she valued Rachel's friendship, a bond that had been forged in the fires of adversity.

One evening, as Lexi sat in her apartment, she received a text from James. Would you like to have dinner with me tomorrow? I'd love to spend some time with you outside of all the chaos.

Lexi's heart fluttered. She had been growing closer to James, and the idea of spending time with him in a more relaxed setting was appealing. She texted back quickly. I'd love that. What time?

The next evening, James picked her up, and they went to a charming little restaurant with a view of the city skyline. The atmosphere was intimate, the dim lighting and soft music creating a perfect backdrop for their evening together.

As they enjoyed their meal, they talked about everything and nothing. Lexi found herself opening up to James in ways she hadn't with anyone else. He listened with genuine interest, his eyes never leaving hers.

After dinner, they took a walk along , as they continued their walk along the river, the city lights shimmering on the water, Lexi felt a deep sense of gratitude for James. His unwavering support had been her anchor during some of the darkest times, and she valued his presence in her life more than she could express.

When James gently took her hand, she felt a warmth that was both comforting and familiar. He stopped, turning to face her, his expression earnest. "Lexi," he began, his voice soft but full of sincerity, "I care about you deeply. I know you've been through so much, and

I just want you to know that I'm here for you, now and always."

Lexi looked into his eyes, seeing the kindness and loyalty that had drawn her to him in the first place. Her heart ached with the weight of what she needed to say, but she knew it was the right thing to do. Taking a deep breath, she spoke, her voice gentle but firm. "James, you've been my rock through everything, and I can't thank you enough for that. But... I'm not ready to jump into another relationship right now. My heart is still healing, and I need time to find myself again."

James's face softened with understanding, though there was a hint of disappointment in his eyes. "I understand, Lexi. Truly, I do. I just want what's best for you."

Lexi reached out and squeezed his hand, giving him a small, appreciative smile. "And that's why I value you so much, James. You've always put me first, and I don't want to lose that. I'd like us to stay friends—good friends. I'm not ready for anything more right now, but your friendship means the world to me."

James nodded, a small smile tugging at the corners of his lips. "I can respect that, Lexi. I'm happy to be here for you.

Lexi continued her therapy sessions with Dr. Carter, each one helping her heal a little more. She also began to volunteer at a local shelter, finding solace in helping others who were struggling.

One day, as she was helping serve lunch at the shelter, she saw a familiar face walk in. It was a young woman who had worked for Beckett, one of the many lives he had touched. The woman looked lost, her eyes filled with pain.

Lexi approached her, offering a warm smile. "Hi, I'm Lexi. Can I help you with something?"

The woman looked up, her eyes wide with surprise. "Lexi? I remember you. You worked for Beckett too."

Lexi nodded, her heart aching for the young woman. "Yes, I did. But I'm not there anymore. What's your name?"

"Maria," the woman replied, her voice barely above a whisper.

Lexi took Maria's hand, leading her to a quiet corner. "Maria, you're not alone. I've been through a lot too, and I want to help you. Let's talk."

As Maria opened up about her struggles, Lexi listened with empathy and understanding. She knew what it was like to feel lost and broken, but she also knew the power of finding support and healing.

Over time, Lexi and Maria formed a strong bond. Lexi became a mentor to Maria, helping her find a job and a place to live. It was a rewarding experience, and it reminded Lexi of how far she had come.

In the weeks that followed, Lexi continued to piece her life back together, navigating the fallout of her past with newfound resilience. Her work with Dr. Carter proved invaluable, each session helping her unravel the layers of trauma and find a path forward. She began to understand that healing wasn't a linear process—it was filled with ups and downs, moments of clarity and confusion.

One afternoon, as she was preparing to leave for another therapy session, she received a call from Detective James.

"Lexi, I have some news for you," he said, his voice serious yet gentle.

"What is it?" Lexi's heart skipped a beat, a sense of apprehension settling over her.

"We've made significant progress in the investigation into Beckett's dealings. It turns out he was involved in a series of high-profile financial crimes that go beyond what we initially uncovered."

Lexi's breath caught in her throat. "What does that mean for us? For me?"

"It means that Beckett's influence is being dismantled, piece by piece. His assets are being frozen, and several of his associates have been taken into custody. It's a significant step forward."

Lexi felt a mixture of relief and sadness. "And Beckett?"

"Beckett has been charged with multiple offenses, including fraud and embezzlement. He's currently awaiting trial."

The news hit Lexi like a tidal wave, leaving her emotions in a whirl. Part of her wanted to feel vindicated, but the truth was that seeing Beckett face consequences didn't erase the pain of their relationship. It was a reminder of the complexity of human emotions—how love and betrayal could coexist in such a painful dance.

The following week, Lexi decided to visit the small bookstore she had come to love. The familiar scent of old paper and ink was a comforting presence, and she found solace in browsing the shelves. As she wandered through the aisles, she spotted a familiar face.

It was Rachel, Beckett's former assistant, standing at the counter with a stack of books. Rachel looked up, her eyes meeting Lexi's.

"Lexi," Rachel said softly, her voice tinged with a mix of regret and hope.

"Rachel," Lexi replied, her tone neutral. "I didn't expect to see you here."

Rachel nodded, a hint of a smile on her lips. "I've been trying to move on, just like you. I wanted to thank you for your support during the investigation. It meant a lot to me."

Lexi studied her for a moment, seeing the weariness in her eyes. "I'm glad you're finding a way to move forward. It's not easy, but I hope you're finding some peace."

Rachel's smile grew a bit warmer. "I am. It's been a difficult journey, but I'm learning to forgive myself and find a new path."

Lexi appreciated Rachel's sincerity. "If you ever need someone to talk to, I'm here."

Rachel's eyes softened. "Thank you, Lexi. I'll keep that in mind."

As they parted ways, Lexi felt a sense of closure. Forgiveness was a powerful tool, one she had learned to wield with care. It was a testament to her growth and resilience.

Later that day, Lexi found herself sitting in a cozy café, sipping a latte and reflecting on her journey. The hustle and bustle of Manhattan continued around her, a reminder of the world moving forward despite her struggles.

The door opened, and Detective James walked in, his face lighting up when he saw Lexi seated at a small café table by the window.

He made his way over, exchanging a warm smile with her before taking a seat across from her.

"How are you doing?" he asked gently, his eyes searching hers for any sign of distress.

"Better," Lexi replied with a small nod. "I've been doing a lot of reflecting, trying to move forward."

James nodded, his expression softening. "I'm glad to hear that, Lexi. You've been through so much, and I've been thinking a lot about us."

Lexi's brow furrowed slightly, her curiosity piqued. "What do you mean?"

James took a deep breath, his gaze steady and sincere. "We've been through so much together, and I care about you more than I can say. I've started to wonder if there could be something more between us. I want us to have a future, Lexi, if you're open to it."

Lexi's heart tightened at his words. She cared deeply for James—he had been her rock, her constant support through everything. But as much as she wanted to, she knew she wasn't ready for another relationship, not so soon. The memories of Beckett were still fresh, still raw, and she couldn't ignore the lingering feelings she had for him.

"James," she began, her voice soft yet firm, "I care about you so much, and I'm incredibly grateful for everything you've done for me. You've been there when I needed someone the most, and I can't thank you enough for that."

James's hopeful expression began to falter as he listened to her, sensing where the conversation was headed.

"But," Lexi continued, "I'm not ready to jump into another relationship right now. I still have feelings for Beckett, and as much as I want to move on, I'm not there yet. I don't want to start something with you when I'm still connected to my past. It wouldn't be fair to either of us."

James looked down for a moment, processing her words. When he met her gaze again, his eyes were understanding, though tinged with disappointment. "I understand, Lexi. I do. I don't want to pressure you into anything you're not ready for."

Lexi reached across the table, taking his hand in hers. "Thank you, James. I just need time to focus on my therapy, to heal, and to figure out what's next for me. I'd like us to stay friends if that's okay with you. Your friendship means the world to me."

James squeezed her hand gently, a small smile returning to his face. "Of course, Lexi. We'll always be friends. I'm here for you, no matter what."

Lexi felt a sense of relief, knowing that James understood and respected her decision. There was a warmth between them, but it was one of friendship, not romantic love. She appreciated his presence in her life, but she knew that she needed to focus on herself right now.

As they sat together, the conversation shifted to lighter topics, and Lexi felt a weight lift from her shoulders. She was grateful for James, not as a potential partner, but as a true friend who would stand by her side, no matter what.

At that moment, Lexi realized that her journey wasn't about rushing into a new relationship; it was about healing, growing, and finding peace within herself. The following weeks were filled with moments of recovery and new beginnings. Lexi continued her therapy sessions, each one helping her build a stronger foundation for her future. She also began to engage in new activities, finding joy in simple pleasures and rediscovering her passions.

One day, as she walked through Central Park, she saw a group of children playing and families enjoying the sunshine. It was a reminder of the beauty of life and the importance of cherishing each moment.

As she sat on a park bench, she received a call from Dr. Carter.

"Lexi, I wanted to check in and see how you're doing," Dr. Carter said.

"I'm doing well," Lexi replied. "I've been making progress and finding joy in the little things."

"That's wonderful to hear," Dr. Carter said. "Remember, therapeutic is a journey, and it's important to be kind to yourself along the way."

Lexi nodded, feeling a sense of gratitude. "Thank you for everything, Dr. Carter. Your support has been invaluable."

As the conversation ended, Lexi felt a renewed sense of hope. She was learning to embrace the future with an open heart, ready to face whatever came her way.

CHAPTER SEVENTEEN

NEW BEGINNINGS

The sun filtered through the sheer curtains, casting a warm glow over the cozy living room of Lexi's new apartment. Brooklyn Heights had always seemed like a distant dream, a place where she could reconstruct her world away from the shadows of Manhattan. Now, it was her reality—a space filled with light, hope, and the promise of new beginnings.

Lexi sat on her plush couch, a steaming cup of coffee cradled in her hands. She gazed out the window, taking in the breathtaking view of the East River and the Manhattan skyline beyond. The city that once felt suffocating now seemed like a distant backdrop, a reminder of how far she had come.

Her mind wandered back to the tumultuous journey that had brought her here. The fear, the heartbreak, the moments of despair—all had shaped her into the person she was today. But now, those memories felt like distant echoes, replaced by a sense of peace and strength she hadn't known was possible.

A gentle knock on the door pulled her from her reverie. Lexi set down her coffee and walked to the door, opening it to reveal Rachel standing there with a tentative smile. It had been weeks since their last meeting at the bookstore, and Lexi was glad to see her friend.

"Rachel, come in," Lexi said warmly, stepping aside to let her in.

Rachel entered, carrying a small plant in a decorative pot. "I thought this might brighten up your new place," she said, handing it to Lexi.

Lexi's eyes softened as she took the plant. "Thank you, Rachel. It's perfect."

They settled in the living room, the plant now taking pride of place on a side table. Rachel looked around, taking in the cozy decor and the sense of calm that filled the space.

"This place suits you, Lexi," Rachel said, her voice filled with genuine warmth. "You look happier, more at peace". Lexi smiled, her heart swelling with gratitude. "I am, Rachel. Moving here was the best decision I could have made. It feels like a fresh start."

Rachel nodded, a thoughtful expression on her face. "You've been through so much, and yet you've come out stronger. It's inspiring."

Lexi reached out and squeezed Rachel's hand. "Thank you. And thank you for being there for me, even when things were tough. Your support means more to me than you'll ever know."

Rachel's eyes glistened with unshed tears. "You're a true friend, Lexi. I'm so glad we reconnected."

As they sat together, sharing stories and laughter, Lexi felt a sense of contentment wash over her. This was what life was meant to be—filled with love, friendship, and moments of genuine connection. She realized that her journey was far from over, but she was ready to embrace whatever came next with an open heart.

Later that afternoon, Lexi took a stroll through the charming streets of Brooklyn Heights. The tree-lined avenues and historic brownstones felt like a world apart from the chaos of Manhattan. She walked with a

New found sense of purpose, taking in the sights and sounds of her new neighborhood.

She passed by a quaint little bakery, the aroma of freshly baked bread and pastries wafting through the air. Unable to resist, she stepped inside, greeted by the warm smile of the baker behind the counter.

"Welcome! What can I get for you today?" the baker asked cheerfully.

Lexi scanned the display case, her eyes landing on a decadent-looking chocolate croissant. "I'll have one of those, please," she said, pointing to the pastry.

As she waited for her order, she struck up a conversation with the baker, learning about the history of the bakery and the community it served. It was these small interactions that made her feel truly at home in Brooklyn Heights.

With her croissant in hand, Lexi continued her walk, savoring each bite as she explored her new surroundings. She discovered a charming park with a view of the river, where she sat on a bench and reflected on her journey.

That evening, Lexi returned to her apartment, the golden glow of the sunset casting a serene light over the room. She sat at her small writing desk, a blank journal open before her. Writing had always been a source of solace for her, a way to process her thoughts and emotions.

She picked up her pen and began to write, her words flowing effortlessly onto the page. She wrote about her fears and triumphs, the people who had supported her, and the lessons she had learned along the way. With each word, she felt a sense of catharsis, as if she were releasing the weight of the past and making room for the future.

The next day, Lexi received a call from Detective James. His voice, steady and reassuring, was a reminder of the strength and support he had provided throughout her ordeal.

"Lexi, I wanted to check in and see how you're doing," he said, his tone warm.

"I'm doing well, James," Lexi replied, a smile in her voice. "I've settled into my new place, and things are looking up."

"That's great to hear," James said. "I also wanted to update you on the investigation. Beckett's trial is moving forward, and we're confident that justice will be served."

Lexi felt a sense of relief wash over her. "Thank you, James. Knowing that helps me find closure."

James's voice softened. "You've shown incredible strength, Lexi. I'm proud of you."

Tears welled in Lexi's eyes, but they were tears of gratitude. "Thank you, James. Your support has meant the world to me."

As weeks turned into months, Lexi continued to rebuild her life, one step at a time. She found a job at a local nonprofit organization, where she used her skills and passion to make a difference in her community. The work was fulfilling and gave her a sense of purpose she hadn't felt in a long time.

One evening, after a particularly rewarding day at work, Lexi sat on her balcony, a glass of wine in hand. The city lights twinkled in the distance, and she felt a profound sense of peace. She thought about the journey that had brought her here—the trials, the heartbreak, and the moments of joy.

Her phone buzzed with a message from Rachel: Let's meet for coffee tomorrow.

Lexi smiled and quickly replied: I'd love that. See you at our usual spot.

The next morning, Lexi met Rachel at a cozy café near her apartment. They chatted over lattes, their conversation filled with laughter and shared dreams. Rachel had also started a new chapter in her life, finding fulfillment in her work and personal growth.

"You know, Lexi," Rachel said, her eyes sparkling with excitement, "I've been thinking about starting my own business. Something that combines my love for books and community."

Lexi's face lit up. "That's an amazing idea, Rachel! You have such a passion for both. What kind of business are you thinking about?"

"A bookstore café," Rachel replied, her smile widening. "A place where people can come together, enjoy good books, and connect over coffee."

Lexi felt a surge of excitement for her friend. "That sounds perfect. I know you'll make it a success."

Rachel reached across the table and squeezed Lexi's hand.

"Thank you, Lexi. Your support means everything to me."

As Lexi walked back to her apartment, she felt a renewed sense of purpose. She had come a long way from the shadows of her past, and she was ready to embrace the future with open arms.

That evening, she received a call from her therapist, Dr. Carter. They spoke about her progress and the steps she had taken to begin again.

"Lexi, I'm so proud of you," Dr. Carter said. "You've shown incredible resilience and strength."

"Thank you, Dr. Carter," Lexi replied, her voice filled with gratitude. "Your guidance has been invaluable."

"Remember, therapeutic is a journey," Dr. Carter said. "Continue to be kind to yourself and take things one day at a time."

Lexi nodded, feeling a sense of calm. "I will. Thank you for everything."

As the call ended, Lexi felt a deep sense of appreciation for the people who had supported her along the way. She knew that her journey was far from over, but she was ready to face whatever came next with courage.

One weekend, Lexi decided to take a trip to the beach. The sound of the waves and the feel of the sand beneath her feet were soothing, a reminder of the beauty and tranquility that life could offer.

As she walked along the shore, she reflected on her journey—the pain and the recovery, the losses and the gains. She realized that every step had led her to this moment, a place of peace and possibility.

She found a quiet spot and sat down, letting the sound of the ocean wash over her. With her journal in hand, she began to write, capturing her thoughts and feelings. It was a moment of introspection and gratitude, a chance to honor her past and embrace her future.

That evening, as Lexi watched the sunset over the ocean, she felt a profound sense of closure. She knew that her journey would continue, but she was ready to face it with an open heart and a spirit of resilience.

As the sky turned shades of pink and orange, Lexi whispered a silent thank you to the universe. She had

found her way through the darkness, and now, she was ready to embrace the light. With a heart full of hope and a spirit of determination, Lexi looked to the future. She knew that there would be challenges ahead, but she was ready to face them, knowing that she was stronger than ever.

In the end, it wasn't just about surviving—it was about thriving, finding joy in the journey, and creating a life filled with love and possibility. And Lexi was ready to do just that, one step at a time.

The sun dipped below the horizon, casting a golden glow over the ocean. Lexi stood up, feeling a sense of peace wash over her. She walked back along the shore, each step a testament to her strength and resilience.

As she made her way home, she knew that she was ready for whatever came next. For she had found her way through the darkness and into the light, and she was ready to embrace the future with open arms.

With a heart full of hope and a spirit of determination, Lexi knew that she was ready to face whatever challenges lay ahead. For she had found her way back to herself, and that was the greatest victory of all.

And so, with each step, Lexi moved forward, ready to embrace the new beginnings that awaited her. In the end, it was about finding the strength to move forward, to heal, and to create a life filled with love, joy, and possibility. And Lexi was ready to do just that.

CHAPTER EIGHTEEN

UNFINISHED BUSINESS

Lexi woke to the soft hum of her phone vibrating on the nightstand. Groggy and still wrapped in the comfort of her dreams, she reached out blindly and grabbed it. The screen glowed in the early morning darkness, displaying a message from an unknown number. The subject line, stark and chilling, read "Unfinished Business."

She sat up, her heart pounding in her chest. The tranquility of her new life in Brooklyn Heights suddenly felt fragile. Her mind raced as she opened the message.

"We need to talk. There are things you don't know. Meet me tonight at the café on Elm Street. Come alone."

Lexi's pulse quickened. The café on Elm Street was a quiet, nondescript place, far from the chaos of Manhattan. She had visited it once, enjoying a peaceful afternoon with a book. But now, the thought of returning there filled her with unease.

Who could this be? What could they possibly want? The questions swirled in her mind, pulling her back into the shadows she had worked so hard to escape. She took a deep breath, trying to calm herself. She had faced worse and come out stronger. This was just another hurdle, another test of her resilience.

The day passed in a blur. At work, Lexi struggled to focus, her mind constantly drifting back to the message. Her colleagues noticed her distraction, but she brushed off their concerns with a forced smile and a vague excuse about not sleeping well. Inside, she felt the weight of the unknown pressing down on her, a constant reminder that her past was not as far behind her as she had hoped.

That evening, she stood in front of her closet, debating what to wear. She needed to project confidence and strength, even if she felt anything but. She chose a simple yet elegant outfit—a black blouse paired with dark jeans and ankle boots. Practical, yet sophisticated. As she applied her makeup, she caught her reflection in the mirror. Her eyes, usually so full of determination, now held a hint of fear. She shook her head, steeling

herself for whatever lay ahead. This was her life, and she was done letting anyone else control it.

The café on Elm Street was dimly lit, its warm, inviting atmosphere a stark contrast to the turmoil in Lexi's heart. She arrived early, choosing a table in the corner where she could see the entrance. The barista, a friendly young woman with a bright smile, took her order—a chamomile tea, something to soothe her nerves.

Lexi waited, her eyes constantly darting to the door every time it opened. The minutes ticked by slowly, each one amplifying her anxiety. She sipped her tea, the warmth doing little to calm her.

Finally, the door swung open, and a figure stepped inside. Lexi's breath caught in her throat. It was a man, tall and broad-shouldered, his face obscured by a hat. He scanned the room, his eyes landing on her. He approached, his steps deliberate and measured.

"Lexi?" he asked, his voice low and cautious.

She nodded, her heart racing. "Yes. Who are you?"

He removed his hat, revealing a face that was both familiar and foreign. "My name is Marcus. I worked with Beckett."

Lexi's eyes widened. "Worked with him? What do you mean?"

Marcus sat down, his expression serious. "I was his security chief. But there's more to the story than you know. Beckett had a lot of enemies, and not all of them are gone."

Lexi leaned forward, her curiosity piqued despite her fear. "What are you talking about? Beckett's in jail. It's over."

Marcus shook his head. "No, Lexi. It's not over. There are people out there who were involved in his schemes. Dangerous people. And they're not happy that you helped bring him down."

A chill ran down Lexi's spine. She had suspected that Beckett's reach extended beyond what she knew, but hearing it confirmed was terrifying. "What do they want from me?"

"To be honest, I'm not entirely sure," Marcus admitted. "But I know they're watching you. They see you as a threat. That's why I reached out. You need to be careful."

Lexi's mind raced. The thought of being watched, of still being in danger, was almost too much to bear. "What should I do?"

Marcus leaned closer, his eyes intense. "You need to stay vigilant. Trust no one. And most importantly, don't let your guard down. These people are ruthless."

Lexi nodded, her resolve hardening. She had faced danger before and come out stronger. She could do it again. "Thank you, Marcus. For warning me."

He stood up, placing a hand on her shoulder. "Take care, Lexi. And remember, you're not alone. There are still people who want to see justice served."

As Marcus left the café, Lexi sat back, her mind reeling. She had thought her ordeal was over, but it seemed it was just beginning. She finished her tea, the warmth now a comfort rather than a distraction. She would face this new threat head-on, just as she had faced everything else. She was stronger than her past, and she would not let it define her.

The next morning, Lexi woke with a renewed sense of purpose. The encounter with Marcus had shaken her, but it had also ignited a fire within her. She was done being a victim. She would take control of her life and ensure her safety.

She spent the day meticulously going over her apartment, checking for any signs of surveillance. It was a tedious and nerve-wracking task, but it gave her a sense of control. She found nothing, but the act itself was empowering. She would not be caught off guard.

That afternoon, she called Rachel, asking her to come over. She needed to confide in someone she trusted, and Rachel had proven to be a true friend. When Rachel arrived, Lexi wasted no time in explaining the situation.

Rachel's eyes widened with concern. "Lexi, this is serious. Are you sure you're okay?"

"I'm fine, Rachel," Lexi reassured her. "But I need to be vigilant. And I need your help."

Rachel nodded, her expression resolute. "Of course. Whatever you need."

Together, they devised a plan. Lexi would continue to go about her daily life but with added precautions. She would change her routines, avoid predictable patterns, and always stay aware of her surroundings. Rachel would act as an extra set of eyes, watching for anything suspicious.

The days turned into weeks, and Lexi slowly adjusted to her new reality. She remained cautious, but she refused to let fear control her. She continued to work, finding solace in the routine and the sense of purpose it gave her.

One evening, as she was walking home from the subway station, she felt a presence behind her. Her heart raced, but she forced herself to remain calm. She glanced over her shoulder, her eyes scanning the street.

A figure lurked in the shadows, watching her. Lexi quickened her pace, her mind racing. She ducked into a nearby store, her breath coming in short, panicked gasps. She waited, her eyes fixed on the entrance.

Minutes passed, and the figure did not follow. Lexi breathed a sigh of relief, but the encounter left her shaken. She called Rachel as soon as she got home, needing to hear a familiar voice.

"Rachel, I think someone was following me," she said, her voice trembling.

Rachel's voice was filled with concern. "Are you safe now?"

"Yes, I'm home. But it scared me."

"Lexi, maybe you should talk to Detective James. He can help you."

Lexi nodded, realizing that Rachel was right. She couldn't handle this alone. She needed professional help.

The next day, Lexi met with Detective James at a quiet café. She explained everything, from the mysterious message to the encounter with Marcus and the figure that had followed her.

James listened intently, his expression serious. "Lexi, this is very concerning. We'll need to take extra precautions to ensure your safety."

"What should I do?" Lexi asked, her voice filled with uncertainty.

"For starters, we'll increase patrols around your neighborhood," James said. "And I'd advise you to

consider some form of personal protection, like self-defense classes or even a security system for your apartment."

Lexi nodded, feeling a sense of relief. "Thank you, James. I appreciate your help."

James reached across the table, his hand covering hers. "We'll get through this, Lexi. You're not alone."

The weeks that followed were a blur of heightened security measures and cautious living. Lexi took self-defense classes, learning how to protect herself in case of an attack. She installed a state-of-the-art security system in her apartment, complete with cameras and alarms.

Despite the precautions, the sense of being watched never fully left her. She remained vigilant, always aware of her surroundings. But she refused to let fear control her life. She continued to work, to see friends, to live as normally as possible.

One evening, as she was reviewing some documents for work, her phone buzzed with a new message. Her heart skipped a beat as she saw it was from the unknown sender again.

"You're not safe. We need to talk. Meet me at the same place tomorrow night. Come alone."

Lexi's hands trembled as she read the message. The fear that she had managed to keep at bay surged to the surface. She took a deep breath, trying to calm herself. She needed to think clearly.

She called Rachel, needing to hear a friendly voice. "Rachel, I got another message. They want to meet again."

Rachel's voice was filled with concern. "Lexi, you can't go alone. It's too dangerous."

"I know," Lexi said, her mind racing. "But I need to find out who this is and what they want. I can't keep living like this."

Rachel sighed. "All right. But you need to be careful. And let Detective James know. He can help you."

Lexi nodded, feeling a sense of determination. "I will. Thanks, Rachel". Lexi arrived at the café on Elm Street the next evening, her heart pounding. She had informed Detective James, and he had assured her that undercover officers would be nearby, ready to intervene if necessary.

She sat at the same table, her eyes scanning the room. She felt a sense of déjà vu, the same mix of fear and anticipation as before. She ordered a chamomile tea, the familiar routine a small comfort.

The door opened, and a figure stepped inside. Lexi's breath caught in her throat as she recognized Marcus. He approached, his expression serious.

"Lexi," he said, sitting down across from her. "Thank you for coming."

"What is this about, Marcus?" Lexi asked, her voice trembling. "Why are you still contacting me?"

Marcus leaned forward, his eyes intense. "Because there's more you need to know. Beckett had connections to people who were still at large. They see you as a threat and won't stop until you're silenced."

Lexi's heart raced. "What can I do?"

"You need to disappear," Marcus said. "Go somewhere safe, where they can't find you. At least until we can take them down."

Lexi shook her head. "I can't just run away. This is my life."

"I know," Marcus said, his voice filled with sympathy. "But your safety is more important. Please, Lexi, trust me. Let me help you."

Tears filled Lexi's eyes. She had fought so hard to rebuild her life, to move forward. The thought of running away, of living in fear, was almost too much to bear.

But she knew Marcus was right. Her safety was paramount. She had to protect herself, no matter the cost.

The next few days were a whirlwind of preparations. Lexi packed her belongings, tying up loose ends at work and saying goodbye to friends. It was a painful process, filled with tears and heartache. But she knew it was necessary.

She found a small, secluded cabin in upstate New York, far from the chaos of the city. It was a quiet, peaceful place, surrounded by nature. A perfect hiding spot.

Rachel helped her with the move, providing emotional support and encouragement. "You'll be okay, Lexi," she said, hugging her tightly. "You're strong. And we'll be here for you, no matter what."

Lexi nodded, tears streaming down her face. "Thank you, Rachel. For everything."

As she settled into her new home, Lexi felt a mix of emotions. Fear, sadness, but also a sense of hope. She had faced so much, and she had survived. She would get through this too.

The days turned into weeks, and Lexi slowly adjusted to her new life. The cabin was a sanctuary, a place of recovery and reflection. She spent her days hiking through the woods, reading, and practicing her self-defense skills.

Despite the solitude, she never felt truly alone. She kept in touch with Rachel and Detective James, their support a constant source of comfort. Marcus checked in regularly, providing updates on the investigation.

One evening, as she sat on the porch, watching the sunset, her phone buzzed with a new message. It was from Marcus.

"We got them. You're safe now". Lexi's heart soared with relief. She had been living in fear for so long, and now, finally, she could breathe again. She called Rachel, her voice filled with joy.

"Rachel, it's over. They got them. I'm safe."

Rachel's voice was filled with happiness. "That's wonderful news, Lexi. I'm so glad."

As Lexi hung up, she felt a sense of peace wash over her. She had faced the darkness and come out stronger. She had found her way through the chaos and into the light.

The next morning, Lexi packed her belongings, ready to return to the city. She felt a mix of emotions—relief, excitement, and a touch of sadness. The cabin had been a place of recovery, a refuge. But now, it was time to move forward.

She arrived in Brooklyn Heights, greeted by the familiar sights and sounds of the city. It felt like coming home. She took a deep breath, feeling a sense of gratitude for the journey she had been on.

As she settled back into her apartment, she reflected on everything she had been through. The pain, the fear, the uncertainty. But also the strength, the resilience, the growth.

She had faced unimaginable challenges and had come out stronger. She had found her way back to herself, and that was the greatest victory of all.

Lexi knew that life would continue to throw challenges her way. But she also knew that she had the strength and the support to face them head-on. She was ready for whatever came next, and she would face it with courage and determination.

CHAPTER NINETEEN

THE FINAL CONFRONTATION

Manhattan's skyline glittered against the night, each building a monument to power and ambition. Lexi's path led her far from the city's gleaming towers, to the stark reality of the county jail where Beckett was awaiting trial. The sterile walls and cold concrete floors of the facility were a world away from the luxury Beckett once controlled, and as Lexi walked through the dimly lit corridors, the gravity of the situation weighed heavily on her.

Her heart pounded as she approached the holding area, each step echoing the finality of this confrontation. She was led to a small, barred room where Beckett stood on the other side of thick glass, his usual confident demeanor dimmed by his circumstances. He turned as she entered, and a flicker of something familiar—a shadow of his old charm—crossed his face.

"Lexi," he greeted her, his voice steady but lacking its former warmth. "I wasn't sure you'd come."

There was an air of surprise in his tone, as though he hadn't expected her to face him here, in this place where his power had been stripped away. Lexi remained standing, the resolve she'd mustered on the way here solidifying. "I had to. We need to talk."

Beckett's smile faded, replaced by a look of guarded curiosity. "Of course. Please, sit."

But Lexi ignored the gesture, refusing to let him dictate the terms of this meeting. "Why, Beckett? Why all the lies, the manipulation?"

He sighed, leaning slightly against the wall behind him, the weight of the truth pressing down on both of them. "It's complicated, Lexi. You wouldn't understand."

"Try me," she replied, her voice steady, her gaze unwavering. "I deserve the truth."

Their eyes locked through the glass, and for a moment, Lexi thought she saw a flicker of regret in Beckett's eyes, a shadow of the man he once was. But just as quickly, it was gone, replaced by the familiar mask he wore so well. "I did what I had to do to protect you. To protect us."

"Protect me?" Lexi's voice rose with incredulity, echoing slightly in the cold, empty room. "You call this protection? You used me, Beckett. You controlled every aspect of my life."

The harsh reality of their situation settled over them like a shroud, the prison walls a stark reminder of the choices that had led them here. Lexi had come for answers, but in this place, stripped of pretense and power, it was clear that the truth was as complicated as the man who now stood before her.

"I was trying to keep you safe!" Beckett's voice was desperate now, his facade cracking. "You have no idea how dangerous this world is, Lexi. I did what I had to do."

Lexi took a step forward, her eyes blazing. "And what about my choice? My freedom? Did you ever consider that maybe I didn't want your protection?"

Beckett looked away, his jaw clenched. "I couldn't take that risk."

Lexi's heart ached at his words. She had loved him, believed in him. But now, she saw him for what he truly was. "You never really loved me, did you? I was just another pawn in your game."

"That's not true!" Beckett's voice was raw with emotion. "I did love you, Lexi. I still do."

"Love?" Lexi's voice was filled with pain. "You don't know the meaning of the word. Love is trust, respect, and freedom. You gave me none of those things."

Beckett took a step towards the glass, his eyes shifting from pleading to calculating. "Lexi, listen to me. My lawyer is already working on getting me out of here. The bail is pending, and it's only a matter of time before I'm free again."

He paused, gauging her reaction, then softened his tone, trying to regain her sympathy. "Please, Lexi. Once I'm out, we can start over. I can change—I will change. Just give me another chance.

"Lexi shook her head, tears streaming down her face. "It's too late, Beckett. I can't live like this anymore. I need to be free. I need to be me."

Beckett's shoulders slumped, his expression one of defeat. "What are you going to do?"

Lexi took a deep breath, her resolve hardening. "I'm leaving. For good this time."

Beckett's eyes widened in shock. "You can't. They'll come after you. They'll hurt you."

"I'll take my chances," Lexi said, her voice steady. "I would rather face the unknown than stay here and be your prisoner."

Beckett's face twisted with anger and desperation. "You don't understand, Lexi. You're mine. You belong to me."

"No, Beckett," Lexi said, her voice firm. "I belong to myself."

With those final words, she turned and walked away, leaving Beckett standing alone. She didn't look back, her heart heavy but resolute. She had faced her demons and confronted the man who had held her captive in his web of lies. And she had emerged stronger, free.

The night air was cool against her skin as Lexi stepped out of the building, the weight of her decision settling on her shoulders. She felt a strange mix of emotions—

relief, fear, sadness. But most of all, she felt a sense of liberation. She was free from Beckett's control, free to live her life on her terms.

She hailed a cab and gave the driver her address. As the city lights blurred past, she allowed herself to breathe, to process everything that had happened. She had faced Beckett, stood up to him, and reclaimed her power. It was a victory, one hard-won and deeply cherished.

Back at her apartment, Lexi felt the silence envelop her. It was a comforting silence, a stark contrast to the chaos of the past few months. She sank onto the couch, exhaustion washing over her. She had done it. She had taken the first step towards reclaiming her life.

Her phone buzzed with a message. It was Rachel, checking in. "How did it go?"

Lexi smiled, a tear slipping down her cheek. "I did it. I confronted him. I'm free."

Rachel's response was immediate. "I'm so proud of you, Lexi. You're stronger than you know."

Lexi wiped her tears, feeling a warmth spread through her. She wasn't alone. She had friends, and people who cared about her. And most importantly, she had herself. She had found her strength, her voice. And she would never let anyone take that away from her again.

The days that followed were a whirlwind of emotions. Lexi felt a sense of peace, of contentment, that she hadn't felt in a long time. She threw herself into her work, finding solace in the routine and the creativity it offered. She spent time with friends, reconnecting with the people who mattered most.

But there were moments of doubt, of fear. She knew that Beckett's influence still lingered, that his reach was long. But she also knew that she was not the same woman she had been. She was stronger, wiser. She would face whatever came her way with courage and determination.

One evening, as Lexi was preparing dinner, her phone rang. It was Detective James. "Lexi, we need to talk."

Lexi set down the knife she was using, already sensing the gravity of the call. "What's wrong?"

"It's about Beckett," James said, his voice heavy with concern. "He's been granted bail."

Lexi's response was steady, though a hint of frustration crept in. "He mentioned it when I went to confront him about some personal matters, but I didn't think it would happen this soon."

James sighed, the frustration clear on his end. "His lawyer found a loophole, something we didn't see coming. The judge approved it this afternoon. I wanted to warn you—he could be out by tomorrow."

Lexi's grip on the phone tightened, but she remained composed. "Thanks for the heads-up, James. I had a feeling something like this might happen, but I didn't expect it to be so soon."

"Neither did we," James replied. "But until we have him back in custody, you need to stay on your guard. We're monitoring the situation closely, but please, be careful."

"I will," Lexi assured him, her voice firm. "I'm not going to let him catch me off guard."

The call ended, and Lexi returned to her dinner preparations, her mind racing. The fear that once paralyzed her had given way to a cold determination.

The following morning was gray and overcast, the city cloaked in a blanket of damp mist. Lexi's morning routine was mechanical, a series of actions performed on autopilot. She dressed quickly, her mind still reeling from the news. She was halfway out the door when a thought struck her.

The penthouse had state-of-the-art security, but Beckett had proven himself capable of bypassing systems with ease. Lexi decided to check her security settings and make sure everything was in order. She headed to her office, where her laptop awaited.

She sat down, her fingers flying over the keyboard as she accessed the security system's controls. The screen showed a series of security logs and real-time camera feeds. Everything seemed normal. Her eyes flickered to a log entry from the previous night—one she didn't recognize.

She froze, her heart pounding. It was a brief entry, noting an unexpected access to the system. Lexi scanned the details and saw that it was marked as a security breach. She had missed it until now, buried among routine updates.

Her pulse quickened. Beckett had been in her system, perhaps scouting for vulnerabilities or just keeping tabs. She felt a surge of anger. No more. She would not be his pawn, not any longer.

That evening, Lexi attended a charity event she had meticulously planned for weeks. The venue sparkled with elegance, from the crystal chandeliers casting warm light over the room to the guests dressed in their finest attire, each one a picture of sophistication. The glitz and glamour of the event were undeniable, yet they stood in stark contrast to the turmoil churning inside her.

Lexi moved through the crowd with practiced grace, her smile perfectly in place, a mask she had learned to wear well. She greeted donors, exchanged pleasantries with socialites, and posed for photographs, all the while keeping the storm of emotions hidden beneath the surface. Her thoughts were never far from Beckett, the memories of their last encounter replaying in her mind like a film she couldn't turn off.

As the evening progressed, she found herself in conversation with a potential client—a wealthy entrepreneur interested in sponsoring the charity. He spoke passionately about his vision, and his plans to make a difference, but Lexi struggled to focus on his words. She nodded at the right moments, laughed at his jokes, and even managed to contribute to the discussion, yet her mind was elsewhere.

The weight of Beckett's influence, the lingering fear, and the uncertainty of what lay ahead pressed down on her. The room, with its laughter and lively chatter, began to feel suffocating. The elegant decor, once a source of pride, now seemed overwhelming, the lights too bright, the music too loud. Lexi could feel her composure slipping, the mask she wore so carefully beginning to crack.

Realizing she needed to escape, Lexi politely excused herself from the conversation. "Please enjoy the rest of the evening," she said with a smile, her voice steady despite the rising tension within her. The client nodded, unaware of the inner battle she was fighting, and Lexi quickly made her way toward the exit.

As she walked through the grand hall, she passed by clusters of guests engaged in animated discussions, their laughter ringing in her ears. But Lexi felt distant as if she were merely a spectator in her own life. The desire to flee grew stronger with each step, the need for solitude and silence becoming overwhelming.

Finally, she reached the doors and stepped outside into the cool night air. The city buzzed around her, but out here, away from the noise and the crowds, Lexi could finally breathe. She stood for a moment, letting the cool breeze calm her racing heart, the tension slowly ebbing away.

Lexi took a deep breath, feeling a sense of relief wash over her. The weight of the evening, of Beckett, of everything, began to lift. She knew she couldn't avoid the challenges ahead, but for now, she was content to simply be—away from the glitz, away from the expectations, and away from the past that had haunted her for so long.

The evening was cool, and the city lights twinkled like distant stars as Lexi strolled through a nearby park. The soft rustling of leaves underfoot and the gentle hum of the city around her created a serene atmosphere, a stark contrast to the turmoil she had faced in recent months. As she walked, she let her thoughts drift, allowing the peace of the moment to envelop her.

She found herself near a small pond, the water reflecting the glowing city skyline. Lexi paused, taking in the quiet beauty of the scene. A light breeze brushed past her, carrying with it the scent of blooming flowers and the distant sound of laughter from a nearby gathering. For the first time in what felt like forever, she allowed herself to fully relax.

After a few more moments of reflection, Lexi decided it was time to head home. She made her way back to her apartment, feeling a newfound sense of clarity and calm. The walk home was peaceful, each step bringing her closer to the sanctuary of her own space.

As she entered her apartment, Lexi felt a wave of comfort wash over her. The familiar surroundings once tinged with the weight of the past, now seemed lighter, more welcoming. She took a deep breath and smiled to herself, feeling a warmth spread through her chest.

Her thoughts were interrupted by a soft knock at the door. She approached cautiously, peering through the peephole. Her heart sank when she saw a figure on the other side—Beckett.

She hesitated before opening the door. Beckett stood there, his face a mask of calm determination. "Lexi," he said, his voice smooth and unyielding. "We need to talk."

She felt a rush of emotions—fear, anger, and a deep sense of betrayal. "There's nothing more to say, Beckett."

Beckett's eyes narrowed slightly. "You don't get to decide that. I've come too far to let you walk away without understanding what's at stake."

Lexi squared her shoulders, trying to muster every ounce of courage she had. "You think you can control me with threats and manipulation? I'm done with that life."

He took a step closer, his presence intimidating. "You don't know what you're saying. I made decisions for us, for our future. Everything I did was for a reason."

Lexi shook her head. "Everything you did was for yourself, Beckett. I'm not your possession or your project. I'm a person with my own life and choices."

Beckett's face darkened, his voice dropping to a dangerous whisper. "You don't understand the full picture. You're making a mistake you'll regret."

The words stung, but Lexi stood her ground. "The only mistake I made was trusting you. I won't let you drag me down any further."

The confrontation was draining, emotionally and physically. Beckett's presence was a constant reminder of the control he had tried to exert over her life. She needed to reclaim her independence, and that meant confronting him head-on.

As Beckett turned and walked away, Lexi felt a mix of relief and dread. She had faced him, stood up for herself, and reaffirmed her commitment to her freedom. But the sense of unease lingered.

Lexi took a deep breath, feeling a sense of calm wash over her. She had faced her fears and had not been broken by them. The struggle was far from over, but she was no longer the same person who had walked into Beckett's world. She had fought hard to regain her life, and she was ready to continue that fight, no matter what lay ahead.

That night, as Lexi lay in bed, she thought about everything that had happened. The events of the past few months had been a tumultuous journey, but she had emerged stronger and more resilient.

Sleep came slowly, her mind racing with thoughts of what the future might hold. But amidst the uncertainty, one thing was clear—Lexi was no longer afraid. She had faced her demons and had found her strength.

CHAPTER TWENTY

BREAKING FREE

You know those moments in life when everything seems to crash down all at once? That's exactly where we find Lexi as she makes the boldest move yet.

The morning air in Manhattan was crisp, a rare respite from the usual summer humidity. Lexi stood at the edge of the terrace of her new, modest apartment in Brooklyn Heights, gazing out at the distant silhouette of the city that had been her home and her cage. Today was the day she would sever the final ties with Beckett Blackwood, the man who had once been her lover, her protector, and ultimately, her greatest adversary.

You could almost feel her nerves, couldn't you? It's like standing on the precipice, knowing that one step forward could mean freedom or a devastating fall. But that's what makes Lexi so compelling—her resilience in the face of such uncertainty.

Lexi took a deep breath, savoring the moment. She had given herself this one minute to feel the weight of what she was about to do, to acknowledge the fear and the

sadness, before setting it aside. She turned back inside, her modest apartment filled with boxes—half unpacked, half waiting for her to decide their fate.

The plan was simple but terrifying. She would go to Beckett's office, hand him her resignation, and walk away from the luxurious world she had known for the past two years. She had no illusions about how difficult this would be. Beckett was not a man who took kindly to losing, especially not when it came to something—or someone—he considered his.

The subway ride into Manhattan felt surreal. Gone were the sleek black cars and personal drivers. Lexi stood among the morning commuters, her heart pounding with a mix of anxiety and determination. She had dressed in a simple, yet professional outfit—a navy blazer over a white blouse, with matching slacks. It was a stark contrast to the high-end designer clothes Beckett had insisted she wear.

Arriving at Blackwood Tower, Lexi took a moment to steady herself. The imposing glass structure loomed above her, a symbol of Beckett's power and influence. But today, she was determined to reclaim her power, to show that she could stand tall without his shadow looming over her.

"Good morning, Ms. Thompson," the receptionist greeted her as she entered the lobby.

"Morning, Jessica," Lexi replied with a polite smile. "I'm here to see Mr. Blackwood."

"Of course, go right up."

The elevator ride to Beckett's office on the top floor seemed to stretch on forever. Each floor passed by in a blur, her mind racing with thoughts of what she would say, and how she would explain her decision. But when the doors finally opened, she took a deep breath and stepped out with newfound resolve.

Beckett's office was a stark contrast to the rest of the building—modern and minimalist, with floor-to-ceiling windows that offered a breathtaking view of the city. He was sitting behind his desk, typing away on his laptop, when she walked in.

"Lexi," he said, looking up with a smile that didn't reach his eyes. "This is a surprise."

She handed him the envelope containing her resignation letter. "I'm leaving, Beckett."

His expression shifted from surprise to confusion, and then to a simmering anger. "What do you mean, you're leaving?"

"I can't do this anymore," she said, her voice steady. "I can't be a part of your world. I need to find my path."

Beckett stood up, his towering figure imposing. "You're making a mistake, Lexi. You don't understand—"

"I understand perfectly," she interrupted, refusing to back down. "I understand that I've been living in a gilded cage, and it's time for me to break free."

The tension in the room was palpable. Beckett's eyes bore into hers, searching for any sign of weakness. But Lexi held her ground, determined not to let him intimidate her.

"Fine," he said finally, his voice cold. "If that's what you want. But don't expect me to make it easy for you."

"I never expected it to be easy," she replied. "But it's worth it."

With that, she turned and walked out of his office, her heart pounding. She had done it. She had taken the first step towards reclaiming her life.

Outside Blackwood Tower, Lexi felt a strange mix of emotions—relief, fear, exhilaration. The world seemed brighter, more vivid. She took a deep breath, savoring the sense of freedom.

Her phone buzzed with a message from Rachel, Beckett's former assistant and one of the few people she could still trust.

Meet me for coffee? We need to talk.

Lexi smiled, grateful for the support. She texted back, agreeing to meet at a small café a few blocks away.

The café was bustling with the mid-morning crowd, but Lexi found a quiet corner where she could collect her thoughts. Rachel arrived a few minutes later, her face etched with concern.

"How are you holding up?" Rachel asked, sliding into the seat opposite her.

"I'm... managing," Lexi replied, taking a sip of her coffee. "It's not easy, but I know I made the right decision."

Rachel nodded. "I heard what happened. Beckett isn't taking it well."

"I didn't expect him to," Lexi said. "But I had to do it. I couldn't keep living like that."

Rachel reached across the table, giving her hand a reassuring squeeze. "You're stronger than you know, Lexi. And you're not alone. We'll figure this out together."

The support from Rachel was a lifeline for Lexi. Over the next few days, she began to rebuild her life, piece by piece. She found a small but cozy apartment in Brooklyn Heights, far from the opulence of her previous life but filled with warmth and comfort that money couldn't buy.

She also started looking for a new job, determined to prove that she could succeed on her terms. It wasn't easy—her association with Beckett had opened many doors, but it had also left her with a reputation that was hard to shake. Still, she pressed on, determined to carve out her path.

One evening, as she was unpacking the last of her boxes, her phone rang. It was Rachel.

"Lexi, I have some news," Rachel said, her voice tinged with excitement. "I spoke to a friend of mine who works at a nonprofit. They're looking for new events coordinator. I mentioned your name, and they're interested."

Lexi's heart skipped a beat. "Really? That's amazing!"

"They'd like to meet you for an interview tomorrow," Rachel continued. "I think this could be a great opportunity for you."

"Thank you, Rachel," Lexi said, her voice filled with gratitude. "I don't know what I'd do without you."

"You'd find a way," Rachel replied with a smile in her voice. "But I'm glad I can help."

The interview the next day went better than Lexi could have hoped. The nonprofit's mission resonated deeply with her, and she felt a renewed sense of purpose as she discussed her ideas and experiences.

A few days later, she received the call she had been waiting for.

"Lexi, we'd like to offer you the position," the voice on the other end said. "Welcome to the team."

Tears of joy filled her eyes as she thanked them, her heart swelling with pride. She had done it. She had

taken control of her life and was building something meaningful.

In the weeks that followed, Lexi threw herself into her new role with passion and determination. She felt a sense of fulfillment she hadn't experienced in a long time. The work was challenging, but it was also incredibly rewarding. She was making a difference, and that meant everything to her.

But even as she flourished in her new life, Beckett's shadow lingered. She knew he was still out there, and the fear that he might try to drag her back into his world was never far from her mind.

One evening, as she was walking home from work, her phone buzzed with a message from an unknown number.

We need to talk. Meet me at our spot.

Lexi's heart raced as she read the message. It was from Beckett. She hadn't heard from him since she had left his office, and now he was reaching out, asking to meet.

She hesitated, the fear and uncertainty creeping back in. But she knew she couldn't keep running forever. She had to face him, confront him one last time, and make it clear that she was done with his games.

The next evening, Lexi found herself standing outside the small, secluded park where they had once shared so many moments. The memories flooded back, but she pushed them aside, focusing on the task at hand.

Beckett was already there, sitting on a bench, his face hidden in the shadows. He looked up as she approached, his expression unreadable.

"Lexi," he said, his voice softer than she remembered. "Thank you for coming."

"I'm not here for pleasantries, Beckett," she replied, her tone firm. "What do you want?"

He sighed, running a hand through his hair. "I wanted to see you, to explain—"

"There's nothing left to explain," she interrupted. "I've made my decision. I'm done with you and your world."

Beckett looked at her, his eyes filled with a mix of sadness and something else she couldn't quite place. "I never meant to hurt you, Lexi. I thought I was protecting you, giving you everything you could ever want."

"You were controlling me," she said, her voice trembling with emotion. "You took away my freedom, my sense of self. I can't live like that."

"I know," he admitted, his voice breaking. "I see that now. But I can't let you go. Not like this."

"You have to," she said, her eyes filling with tears. "I deserve a chance to live my own life, to be happy on my terms."

Beckett stood up, his towering figure casting a long shadow. For a moment, he looked as if he might argue, but then he nodded, a defeated look in his eyes. "You're right. You deserve better than I can give you."

Lexi took a step back, her heart aching. "Goodbye, Beckett."

"Goodbye, Lexi," he whispered, his voice barely audible.

She turned and walked away, each step feeling like a weight lifted from her shoulders. She had done it. She had broken free from Beckett's grasp and was ready to embrace her new life.

The days that followed were a whirlwind of activity. Lexi threw herself into her work, finding solace in the

meaningful tasks and the positive impact she was making. The nonprofit community welcomed her with open arms, and she quickly became an integral part of the team.

She also began to reconnect with old friends and make new ones. For the first time in a long time, she felt a sense of belonging and purpose. Her life was her own, and she was determined to make the most of it.

One evening, as she was sitting on her balcony, watching the sunset over the city, she received a call from Rachel.

"How's it going, Lexi?" Rachel asked, her voice warm and cheerful.

"Better than I could have imagined," Lexi replied, smiling. "I feel like I'm finally where I'm supposed to be."

"I'm so happy for you," Rachel said. "You deserve this."

"Thank you," Lexi said, her heart full. "I couldn't have done it without you."

Rachel laughed. "You would have found a way. But I'm glad I could help."

As they chatted, Lexi felt a sense of peace wash over her. She had faced her fears, confronted her past, and emerged stronger than ever. Her journey wasn't over, but she was ready for whatever came next.

And there you have it. Lexi's journey of breaking free from the grasp of a controlling lover and reclaiming her life. It's not just about the grand gestures, but the quiet moments of resilience and the strength to move forward. She's a testament to the power of determination and the importance of finding one's path.

So, as the city lights flicker on and the world moves forward, Lexi stands tall, ready to embrace the future with open arms. And isn't that what we all strive for? To find our way, to break free from the shadows, and to live a life filled with purpose and love.

CHAPTER TWENTY-ONE

REDEMPTION

The evening sky over Manhattan was painted in hues of pink and gold as Lexi stood at the window of her modest Brooklyn Heights apartment, lost in thought. It had been weeks since her last encounter with Beckett, weeks filled with a sense of newfound freedom and purpose. Yet, tonight, a message had arrived that threw her into a whirlpool of emotions.

Lexi, I need to see you. Please. It's important. - Beckett

She stared at the message, her heart pounding. Beckett had always been able to stir something deep within her—anger, passion, confusion. But now, after everything they had been through, she wasn't sure what she felt anymore.

Her phone buzzed again, and she saw another message from Beckett.

I've changed, Lexi. Give me one chance to prove it.

She hesitated the memories of their tumultuous past playing in her mind. Could she trust him? Could she forgive him? With a deep breath, she made up her mind. She had to see for herself if Beckett was truly capable of redemption.

The journey to Beckett's penthouse was a familiar one, yet it felt different this time. Lexi was no longer the same person who had once been ensnared by Beckett's charm and control. She was stronger, more self-assured. As the elevator ascended to the top floor, she braced herself for what was to come.

The doors opened, and there he was, standing by the floor-to-ceiling windows, his silhouette outlined by the city lights. He turned as she stepped out, his eyes filled with a mixture of optimism and apprehension.

"Lexi," he said softly, taking a step towards her.

She held up a hand, stopping him. "Why did you ask me here, Beckett?"

He sighed, running a hand through his hair. "I know I've hurt you. More than I can ever make up for. But I've spent these past weeks reflecting on my actions, and on who I've become. And I realize now that I was wrong. I don't want to lose you, Lexi. I want to make things right."

His words hung in the air, heavy with emotion. Lexi crossed her arms, her gaze unwavering. "And how do you plan to do that?"

"I've started therapy," he admitted, his voice barely above a whisper. "I'm working through my issues, trying to understand why I felt the need to control everything around me. But more than that, I'm learning how to let go."

She was taken aback by his admission. Beckett, the man who always seemed so in control, was seeking help? It was a start, but it wasn't enough.

"That's a step in the right direction," she said slowly. "But it doesn't erase what you did. You manipulated me, controlled me. How can I trust that you've truly changed?"

He took a deep breath, his eyes pleading. "I know I have to earn your trust again, and I'm willing to do whatever it takes. Just give me a chance, Lexi. One chance to show you that I'm serious."

The sincerity in his voice, the vulnerability in his eyes—it was hard to ignore. Lexi felt a pang of sympathy, but she also knew she had to protect herself.

"Beckett," she began, her voice trembling, "I've been through so much because of you. I've had to rebuild my life from scratch. I can't just forget all that."

"I don't expect you to," he replied quickly. "But I'm not asking you to forget. I'm asking for a chance to make amends. To prove that I can be the man you deserve."

Lexi looked at him, her heart torn. Could she give him that chance? Could she open herself up to the possibility of being hurt again?

"All right," she said finally, her voice steady. "One chance, Beckett. But understand this—if you ever try to control me again, if you ever manipulate me, I'm gone. For good."

A flicker of hope crossed his face. "I promise, Lexi. I'll do everything I can to make this right."

They stood there, the silence between them charged with unspoken words and emotions. Beckett took a tentative step forward, and when she didn't move away, he closed the distance between them, taking her hand in his.

"I missed you," he said softly, his thumb gently caressing her palm.

Lexi felt a shiver run through her at his touch. Despite everything, the connection between them was undeniable. She looked up into his eyes, searching for any sign of deceit, but all she saw was sincerity and remorse.

"I missed you too," she admitted, her voice barely above a whisper.

Beckett's eyes softened, and he leaned in, his lips brushing against hers in a tender kiss. It was a kiss filled with promise, a vow to be better, to love her the way she deserved.

Over the next few weeks, Beckett made good on his promise. He attended therapy sessions diligently, often sharing his progress with Lexi. He opened up to her in ways he never had before, revealing the fears and insecurities that had driven his need for control.

Lexi, in turn, found herself opening up to him as well. They spent long nights talking, sharing their desires and dreams, their fears and regrets. Slowly but surely, the walls between them began to crumble, and they started to rebuild their relationship on a foundation of trust and mutual respect.

One evening, as they sat on the terrace of Beckett's penthouse, looking out over the city, he turned to her, his expression serious.

"Lexi, there's something I need to say," he began, taking her hand in his. "I know I've put you through hell, and I can never fully make up for that. But I want you to know that I love you. Truly, deeply. And I'm committed to being the man you deserve."

Her heart swelled with emotion at his words. "I love you too, Beckett. But we have to take this one step at a time. Trust isn't rebuilt overnight."

"I understand," he said, his voice filled with determination. "And I'm willing to take it as slowly as you need. As long as it means I get to be with you."

They sat there in silence, the weight of his words settling over them. For the first time in a long time, Lexi felt a sense of hope. Maybe, just maybe, they could make this work.

The days turned into weeks, and as they navigated the complexities of their relationship, they found themselves growing closer than ever. Beckett continued his therapy, and Lexi saw the changes in him—he was more patient, and more understanding, and most importantly, he respected her boundaries.

One evening, as they were cooking dinner together, Beckett turned to her, a playful smile on his lips.

"Remember that time we tried to make pasta, and it ended up everywhere except the plate?" he asked, his eyes twinkling with amusement.

Lexi laughed, the memory flooding back. "How could I forget? You were so determined to impress me, and instead, we ended up with a kitchen disaster."

"I'd say it was a success," he replied, wrapping his arms around her from behind. "After all, it led to our first kiss."

She leaned back against him, a contented smile on her face. "I suppose you're right."

Their evenings were filled with moments like these—simple, yet profound. They cooked together, watched movies, and took long walks through the city. They learned to enjoy each other's company without the weight of their past mistakes hanging over them.

But despite the progress they had made, Lexi knew that the real test would come when Beckett faced a crisis. How he handled it would determine if he had truly changed.

That test came sooner than expected.

One afternoon, Beckett received a call from his lawyer. His company was facing a major lawsuit, and the stress was palpable. Lexi watched as he listened intently, his expression growing more tense by the second.

When he hung up, he turned to her, a storm of emotions in his eyes. "They're trying to bring us down, Lexi. This could ruin everything I've worked for."

She reached out, taking his hand in hers. "We'll get through this, Beckett. Together."

He sighed, running a hand through his hair. "I just... I don't know how to handle this."

"Take it one step at a time," she said gently. "Remember what you've learned in therapy. You don't have to control everything. Just focus on what you can do, and let the rest go."

He nodded, taking a deep breath. "You're right. I can't let this consume me."

Over the next few days, Lexi stood by his side as he navigated the crisis. She watched as he dealt with his lawyers, made difficult decisions, and managed the stress without reverting to his old ways. It wasn't easy, but he did it, and she couldn't have been prouder.

One evening, after a particularly grueling day, Beckett turned to her, his eyes filled with gratitude.

"Thank you for being here, Lexi," he said, his voice thick with emotion. "I don't know what I would have done without you."

"You don't have to thank me," she replied, wrapping her arms around him. "We're in this together."

He held her close, his heart full. "I love you, Lexi. More than anything."

"I love you too, Beckett," she whispered, her eyes filled with tears. "And I'm so proud of you."

Their love had been tested, but it had emerged stronger than ever. They had faced their demons, confronted their past, and found a way to move forward. And as they stood together, looking out over the city, they knew that whatever the future held, they would face it together.

In that moment, Lexi realized that love wasn't about grand gestures or perfect moments. It was about the quiet strength that came from standing by each other's side, no matter what. It was about forgiveness, growth, and the willingness to fight for what truly mattered.

CHAPTER TWENTY-TWO

LOVE IN THE LUXURY LANE

The early morning light filtered through the large windows of Beckett's penthouse, casting a warm glow over the sleek, modern furniture. Lexi stood by the window, gazing at the Manhattan skyline, a sense of peace settling over her. This city had been the backdrop for so much of her turmoil, but now, it felt like the start of something new.

Behind her, Beckett stirred, waking up to find the bed beside him empty. He propped himself up on one elbow, watching her momentarily before calling out softly, "Penny for your thoughts?"

Lexi turned, a soft smile playing on her lips. "Just thinking about how far we've come."

Beckett got out of bed and walked over to her, wrapping his arms around her from behind. "It's been quite the journey, hasn't it?"

She leaned back into him, savoring the warmth of his embrace. "Yes, it has. But I wouldn't change a thing. Every challenge, every struggle—it's all led us to this moment."

He turned her around to face him, his eyes searching hers. "Are you happy, Lexi?"

She looked up at him, her heart swelling with emotion. "Happier than I've ever been. Because I know that no matter what happens, we'll face it together."

His expression softened, and he leaned down to kiss her, a tender, lingering kiss that spoke volumes. When they finally pulled apart, he rested his forehead against hers. "I love you, Lexi."

"I love you too, Beckett."

They stood there for a moment, just holding each other, basking in the quiet intimacy of the morning. It was a new beginning, a chance to build a future free from the shadows of the past.

The day unfolded slowly, a lazy Sunday filled with simple pleasures. They made breakfast together, laughter and teasing filling the kitchen. Beckett, ever the perfectionist, attempted to flip a pancake and ended up with half of it on the counter.

Lexi laughed, her eyes sparkling with amusement. "You know, for a billionaire, you're not very good at this."

He grinned, unfazed by the mess. "That's why I have you. You make everything better."

They ate on the terrace, the city sprawled out beneath them, talking about everything and nothing. It was in these moments that Lexi felt the most content, the most at home. They talked about their dreams, their plans for the future, and the life they wanted to build together.

After breakfast, they decided to extend their day with a visit to a nearby luxury resort. The ambiance was serene, with lush gardens, sparkling fountains, and private cabanas offering an escape from the bustling city.

They strolled through the resort's elegant pathways, hand in hand, surrounded by the scent of blooming jasmine and the soothing sound of trickling water. The resort's beauty was unmatched, with every corner designed to evoke a sense of peace and indulgence. Lexi couldn't help but feel that their world had transformed into a paradise where time seemed to slow down.

As they approached a secluded area by the resort's infinity pool, Beckett guided her to a private cabana draped in flowing white curtains. Inside, the cabana was adorned with plush cushions and soft, flickering candles, creating an intimate and romantic atmosphere. The horizon stretched endlessly before them, the sun beginning to dip, painting the sky in shades of gold and pink.

Beckett turned to her, his eyes reflecting the warmth of the setting sun. "Lexi," he began, his voice filled with emotion, "I've been thinking a lot about us, about everything we've been through. And I realized that I don't want to spend another moment without knowing our future is sealed."

Lexi's breath caught as she gazed at him, her heart fluttering with anticipation. Beckett reached into his pocket and pulled out a small, velvet box. As he opened it, a stunning ring, with a diamond that caught the light and shimmered like the stars above, was revealed.

"Lexi," he said, his voice thick with emotion, "will you marry me?"

Tears welled up in Lexi's eyes as she looked at him, every ounce of love she felt for him flooding her heart. This moment, in this place, felt like a dream. "Yes, Beckett," she whispered, her voice trembling with happiness. "Yes, I'll marry you."

Beckett gently slipped the ring onto her finger, his touch tender and full of promise. Lexi threw her arms around him, holding him close as tears of joy streamed down her face. They kissed, their embrace filled with love and a shared promise of a future together.

As they pulled back, their foreheads resting against each other, Lexi felt the world around her fade away, leaving only the two of them in their perfect moment. The sun dipped below the horizon, the sky now a canvas of deep purples and soft oranges, as they sat together in the cabana, savoring the beginning of their new journey.

Finally, after what felt like an eternity of bliss, they decided to return to their apartment. The luxury of the day, the emotions they had shared, and the love that had been reaffirmed between them made the evening unforgettable. They walked back to their apartment, hand in hand, knowing that their future was as bright and beautiful as the day they had just experienced.

Back at the penthouse, they curled up on the bed, wrapped in a cozy blanket. Beckett held her close, his fingers gently tracing patterns on her arm.

"I can't believe it," she said softly. "We're doing this."

He kissed the top of her head. "We are. And I promise you, Lexi, I'll spend the rest of my life making you happy."

She looked up at him, her eyes shining. "We'll make each other happy, Beckett. That's what a partnership is about."

That evening, Lexi and Beckett embarked on a lavish adventure that only a billionaire's imagination could conjure.

Beckett had everything meticulously planned, starting with a private helicopter ride that whisked them away to a secluded island retreat, known only to the ultra-wealthy. The chopper soared over the glittering cityscape, and Lexi couldn't help but feel a thrill as the world below became a blur of lights and colors. As they flew, Beckett held her close, his hand warm against the small of her back, his lips brushing her ear as he whispered promises of the night ahead.

When they landed, a luxurious yacht awaited them, its deck adorned with roses and candlelight. The crew discreetly melted into the background as Beckett led Lexi aboard, where a five-star meal was set beneath the stars. The air was filled with the scent of the sea and the soft strains of classical music played by a live quartet. Every detail was designed to delight her senses, but what touched Lexi most was the way Beckett looked at her—as if she were the only woman in the world.

As they dined, their conversation flowed effortlessly, laughter mingling with the gentle sound of the waves. Beckett's gaze never left her, his eyes filled with a warmth that made Lexi's heart flutter. Every word he spoke was laced with affection, every touch was charged with electricity. It was as if the world outside had ceased to exist, leaving only the two of them in this perfect, intimate bubble.

After dinner, Beckett led Lexi to the edge of the deck, where a bed of plush cushions awaited them. They lay together under a canopy of stars, the night air cool against their skin as they nestled into each other. Beckett's hands moved gently over her, each caress a silent declaration of his love. Their kisses grew deeper, more urgent, as the night wore on, their connection palpable in the silence between words.

The yacht gently rocked with the motion of the waves, creating a rhythm that matched the beating of their hearts. Beckett whispered sweet nothings into her ear, his breath warm against her skin. His fingers traced the curve of her cheek, the line of her jaw as if memorizing every inch of her. Lexi felt a surge of emotion, a deep, overwhelming love that made her feel weightless, as though she could float away in his arms.

As the night deepened, the stars above them shone brighter, reflecting in Beckett's eyes as he looked at her with an intensity that took her breath away. "I love you, Lexi," he murmured, his voice thick with emotion. "More than anything in this world."

Lexi smiled, her heart swelling with happiness. "And I love you, Beckett. Forever."

They spent the rest of the night wrapped in each other's arms, their love the only thing that mattered in the world. Every moment felt like a dream, a fairy tale brought to life. The luxury, the romance, the deep connection they shared—it all felt like the culmination of every hope and desire they had ever had.

As dawn began to break, painting the sky in hues of pink and gold, Beckett pulled Lexi closer, pressing a soft kiss to her forehead. "This is just the beginning," he whispered.

Lexi looked up at him, her eyes shining with tears of happiness. "I know," she replied, her voice filled with love. "And I can't wait to see what comes next."

They returned to the city with the first light of day, their hearts full, their bond stronger than ever. It was a night that would forever be etched in their memories, a testament to the power of love, luxury, and the joy of simply being together.

The weeks that followed were a whirlwind of preparations and excitement. They planned a small, intimate wedding, wanting to focus on what truly mattered—their love for each other. Rachel and Emma Lexi's old-time friends assisted and helped with the details, ensuring everything was perfect.

On the wedding day, Lexi stood in front of the mirror, adjusting her dress. It was a simple, elegant gown that made her feel like a princess. She took a deep breath, her heart pounding with anticipation.

Rachel entered the room, her eyes widening in admiration. "You look stunning, Lexi."

Lexi turned a grateful smile on her face. "Thank you, Rachel. For everything."

Rachel hugged her, a rare display of emotion from the usually stoic assistant. "You deserve all the happiness in the world, Lexi."

The ceremony was held in a beautiful garden, the setting sun casting a golden glow over everything. As Lexi walked down the aisle, her eyes locked on Beckett, who stood waiting for her, a look of awe on his face.

When she reached him, he took her hands in his, his eyes filled with love. "You take my breath away," he whispered.

She smiled, her heart full. "You do the same to me."

The officiant began, and as they exchanged vows, there wasn't a dry eye in the audience. They spoke from the heart, their words a testament to the journey they had been on and the love that had brought them here.

"I promise to love you, to support you, and to stand by your side, no matter what," Beckett said, his voice steady and sure. "You are my everything, Lexi."

She looked up at him, tears streaming down her cheeks. "I promise to love you, trust you, and build a life filled with joy and laughter. You are my forever, Beckett."

When the officiant pronounced them husband and wife, they kissed, sealing their vows with a promise of a lifetime of love.

The reception was a joyous celebration, filled with laughter, dancing, and heartfelt toasts. Lexi and Beckett danced under the stars, their first dance as husband and wife a moment of pure magic.

As the night drew to a close, they stood together, looking out at their friends and family. Lexi leaned her head on Beckett's shoulder, a contented sigh escaping her lips.

"This is the beginning of our forever," she said softly.

He kissed her temple, his heart full. "And I can't wait to spend every moment of it with you."

Their love has proven that even the darkest of pasts can lead to the brightest of futures. They've shown us that love is about forgiveness, growth, and the willingness to fight for each other. the belief that love can conquer all, that redemption is always possible, and that true happiness is worth fighting for.

CHAPTER TWENTY-THREE

THE TRUTH REVEALED

Manhattan's skyline is lit up like a Christmas tree, the city's heartbeat pulsing through every street and alley. Now, zoom in on Beckett's penthouse, an opulent fortress of glass and steel perched high above the chaos. It's a place that screams power and wealth, but tonight, it's going to witness something far more profound.

"Lexi stands at the threshold of their penthouse home, her heart a wild drum in her chest. Tonight, the air feels different—charged, like the calm before a storm. She hesitates, her fingers brushing against the cool metal of the door handle. This is it. The moment of truth.

Stepping inside, she's immediately engulfed by the sheer luxury of the place. The marble floors gleam under the soft lighting and the modern art pieces are strategically placed to catch the eye. But Lexi isn't here to admire the decor. She's here to confront the man who has turned her world upside down.

Beckett is in the living room, his tall frame silhouetted against the floor-to-ceiling windows that offer a breathtaking view of the city. He turns as she enters, his expression unreadable. For a moment, they simply stare at each other, the silence between them thick with unspoken words.

"Lexi," Beckett finally says, his voice low and measured. "I didn't expect you so soon."

Lexi takes a deep breath, trying to steady herself. "I need to talk to you, Beckett. About everything."

His eyes darken slightly, but he nods. "All right. Let's sit."

But Lexi remains standing, her gaze fixed on him. "No. I want answers, Beckett. And I want them now."

Beckett sighs, running a hand through his dark hair. He motions for her to follow him to the couch, and reluctantly, she does. They sit facing each other, the tension palpable.

"Okay, Lexi," Beckett says, leaning forward. "What do you want to know?"

She swallows hard, gathering her thoughts. "I found out something today. Something about your past. About why you are the way you are."

Beckett's eyes narrow slightly, a flicker of something—fear?—crossing his face. "What did you find out?"

Lexi takes another deep breath. "I know about your father. About the abuse. About everything he did to you."

For a moment, Beckett is completely still. Then, his shoulders slump, and he looks away, out the window. "I didn't want you to know," he says quietly. "I never wanted you to see that part of me."

Lexi feels a surge of empathy for him, but she pushes it down. She needs to stay strong. "Why didn't you tell me, Beckett? Why keep it a secret?"

He turns back to her, his eyes filled with a pain that cuts deep. "Because it's not something I'm proud of, Lexi. My father was a monster, and I swore I'd never be like him. But... but some things, they stay with you, no matter how hard you try to bury them."

Lexi's heart aches for him, but she's also angry. Angry that he didn't trust her enough to share this with her.

"You should have told me, Beckett. I deserved to know. I could have helped you."

He shakes his head. "I didn't want your pity, Lexi. I wanted you to see me as strong, as someone who could protect you, not someone who needed saving."

Lexi leans forward, her voice softening. "Beckett, loving someone means accepting all parts of them. The good, the bad, and the ugly. I don't pity you. I just... I just want to understand."

Beckett looks at her, his eyes searching her face. "I thought I could protect you by keeping you in the dark. But I see now that I was wrong. I was trying to control everything, just like my father did."

Lexi reaches out, taking his hand in hers. "You're not your father, Beckett. You're not a monster. But you need to let me in. We need to face this together."

For a moment, Beckett is silent, his eyes locked on their joined hands. Then, he nods slowly. "You're right, Lexi. I need to let go of the past if we're ever going to have a future. "They sit there, holding hands, the weight of their shared pain hanging in the air. It's a moment of raw honesty, and it's the first step toward healing.

But Lexi knows this is just the beginning. They have a long road ahead of them, filled with challenges and revelations. But for the first time, she feels a glimmer of hope. Because now, they're facing it together.

And as the city lights twinkle outside, Lexi knows that whatever happens next, they have the strength to face it. Together.

Lexi's heart is heavy, torn between empathy and anger. She stands up, moving to the window, her reflection merging with the city's glittering lights. She has always loved this view, but tonight, it feels bittersweet. She turns back to Beckett, her voice barely above a whisper.

"How did it start, Beckett? The abuse?"

He closes his eyes as if trying to block out the memories. "My father was a powerful man. He had a reputation to uphold. Any sign of weakness was unacceptable. When I was a child, I made the mistake of showing fear, of not living up to his expectations. That's when it began. The beatings, the psychological torment. He wanted to mold me into his image, a man who feared nothing and no one."

Lexi's throat tightens. "And your mother?"

"She tried to protect me, but there was only so much she could do. Eventually, she left, unable to bear the constant violence. I stayed, thinking I could handle it. That I could be strong enough to survive."

Lexi's tears fall freely now, the pain in Beckett's voice tearing at her heart. "You were just a child, Beckett. No one should have to endure that."

He looks at her, his eyes filled with a mixture of sorrow and determination. "I swore I'd never be like him. But in trying to protect you, I became a version of him. Controlling, manipulative. I'm so sorry, Lexi."

She takes a deep breath, trying to process everything. "You have to promise me, Beckett. No more secrets. No more lies. If we're going to move forward, it has to be together, with honesty. "He nods, his expression resolute. "I promise, Lexi. No more secrets."

They sit in silence for a while, the weight of their conversation settling around them. Lexi knows that forgiveness won't come easily, but she's willing to try. Because beneath the layers of pain and mistrust, she still loves Beckett. And love, true love, is worth fighting for.

The next morning, Lexi wakes up to find Beckett already gone. She feels a pang of anxiety, but then she sees the note on the pillow beside her.

"Lexi, I had to step out for a meeting. I'll be back soon. We need to talk more. Love, Beckett."

She sighs, clutching the note to her chest. It's a small gesture, but it means a lot. She gets out of bed, ready to face the day. But as she moves through the penthouse, she can't shake the feeling that something is off.

Her phone buzzes with a message from Rachel, her best friend and confidante.

"How are you holding up, Lexi? Did you talk to him?"

Lexi quickly types a reply. "Yes, we talked. It was intense but necessary. There's still a lot to work through."

Rachel's response is immediate. "you're an incredibly strong lady, And I admire you for it.

Lexi smiles, feeling a bit of comfort. She makes her way to the kitchen, deciding to distract herself with breakfast. But as she opens the fridge, her phone buzzes again. This time, it's an unknown number.

"Hello?"

"Ms. Thompson? This is Detective James. We need to talk."

Lexi's heart skips a beat. "Detective James? What's going on?"

"It's about Beckett. We've discovered some new information, and we need you to come down to the station."

Lexi feels a knot form in her stomach. "I'll be there as soon as I can."

She quickly gets dressed, her mind racing. What could this be about? She grabs her bag and heads out the door, her heart pounding.

At the police station, Detective James greets her with a grim expression. "Thank you for coming, Ms. Thompson. Please, follow me."

They walk to a small, sterile room. Lexi sits down, her anxiety mounting. "Detective, what's this about?"

James sits opposite her, his eyes serious. "We've been investigating Beckett's father, John Carter. New evidence has come to light that implicates him in several illegal activities, including money laundering and embezzlement. But that's not all."

Lexi's mind reels. "What else?"

"We've also uncovered evidence that suggests Beckett may have been involved, albeit unknowingly, in some of his father's schemes. We're not saying he's guilty, but we need to question him further."

Lexi feels a cold dread settle over her. "Beckett had no idea. He was just a child when all this happened."

James nods. "We believe you. But we need to get to the bottom of this. For Beckett's sake as well as everyone else's."

Lexi leaves the station in a daze. How much more can they endure? She needs to find Beckett, to warn him. But as she steps outside, she sees him standing by his car, waiting for her.

"Beckett!" she calls out, rushing to him. "We need to talk."

He looks at her, concern etched on his face. "Lexi, what's wrong?"

She takes his hand, pulling him close. "The police have new evidence about your father. They think you might have been involved in his illegal activities."

Beckett's face pales. "What? That's impossible. I didn't know anything about his business dealings."

Lexi holds his gaze, her voice firm. "I believe you, Beckett. But we need to figure this out together. We can't let your father's past destroy our future."

Beckett nods, his jaw set. "You're right. We need to clear my name. And we need to do it together."

They head back to the penthouse, their minds racing with possibilities. As they step inside, Beckett turns to Lexi, his expression resolute. "No more secrets. No more lies. We face this head-on, together."

Lexi nods, feeling a surge of determination. "Together."

The next few days are a whirlwind of meetings with lawyers, conversations with detectives, and late-night strategy sessions. Lexi and Beckett work tirelessly to uncover the truth, their bond growing stronger with each passing day.

One evening, as they sit in the living room surrounded by documents and notes, Beckett looks at Lexi, his eyes filled with gratitude. "I don't know what I'd do without you, Lexi. You've been my rock through all of this."

She smiles, reaching out to touch his hand. "And you've been mine, Beckett. We're in this together. No matter what."

As they continue their investigation, they uncover a trail of deceit that stretches back years. It becomes clear that John Carter had been involved in some very shady dealings, but Beckett's involvement was minimal and unintentional. They gather the evidence needed to clear his name, but the process is long and grueling.

Throughout it all, Lexi and Beckett find moments of solace in each other's arms. They share stories, laugh at old memories, and even manage to steal a few romantic moments amidst the chaos. Their love, tested and tried, becomes a beacon of hope in the darkness.

One night, as they sit on the rooftop terrace, looking out over the city, Beckett pulls Lexi close. "I know this hasn't been easy, Lexi. But you've shown me what real strength and love look like. I promise you, once this is over, we'll build the life we've always dreamed of. "Lexi looks up at him, her eyes shining with determination.

"We will, Beckett. Because we have each other. And together, we can overcome anything."

As the investigation nears its conclusion, the truth about John Carter's crimes comes to light. Beckett is exonerated, his name cleared. It's a victory hard-won, but it brings with it a sense of closure and a new beginning.

Standing in the courtroom on the final day, Lexi feels a wave of relief washes over her. Beckett takes her hand, squeezing it gently. "We did it, Lexi. We made it through."

She smiles up at him, her heart full. "Yes, we did. And now, we can finally move forward."

Back at the penthouse, they celebrate with a quiet dinner, just the two of them. Beckett raises his glass, his eyes locking with Lexi's. "To us. To our future."

Lexi clinks her glass with his, feeling a sense of peace she hasn't felt in a long time. "To us."

As they sit together, enjoying the moment, Lexi knows that their journey is far from over.

CHAPTER TWENTY-FOUR

FOREVER FREE

The morning light seeped into Beckett's penthouse, casting a warm, golden glow over the opulent decor. The world outside was waking up, but inside, a different kind of awakening was taking place. Lexi stood by the floor-to-ceiling windows, looking out over the sprawling cityscape of Manhattan. The view was breathtaking, but her thoughts were far from the bustling streets below.

"Good morning," came Beckett's voice, soft and filled with a tentative desire. He approached her slowly, as if afraid to shatter the fragile peace they had found.

Lexi turned to face him, her heart swelling with a mix of emotions. The journey they had been on was tumultuous, filled with pain, revelations, and growth. But standing there, in the quiet of the morning, she felt a sense of calm she hadn't experienced in a long time.

"Morning," she replied, her voice gentle. She reached out, taking his hand in hers. The connection between them felt stronger than ever, a bond forged through fire and tempered by understanding.

Beckett's eyes searched hers, looking for any sign of lingering doubt. "How are you feeling?" he asked, his thumb brushing lightly over her knuckles.

Lexi took a deep breath, considering her words. "I feel... different," she said finally. "Lighter, maybe. Like a weight has been lifted."

Beckett nodded, his expression softening. "I know what you mean. It's been a long road, but we're here. Together."

They stood there for a moment, the silence between them comfortable and full of unspoken promises. The events of the past months had tested them in ways neither could have imagined. But they had emerged stronger, more resilient, and with a deeper understanding of themselves and each other.

"Do you want to go for a walk?" Beckett suggested, his voice breaking the quiet. "I think some fresh air might do us good."

Lexi smiled a genuine, heartfelt smile that reached her eyes. "I'd love that."

They left the penthouse hand in hand, stepping out into the crisp morning air. The streets of Manhattan were alive with energy, the sounds of the city a comforting backdrop to their thoughts. They walked in silence for a while, each lost in their reflections.

"Do you remember the first time we met?" Beckett asked suddenly, a wistful note in his voice.

Lexi chuckled softly. "How could I forget? You were the enigmatic billionaire, and I was the starry-eyed event planner who couldn't believe my luck."

Beckett squeezed her hand gently. "I was captivated by you from the start. Your passion, your drive, the way you lit up a room… it was impossible not to be drawn to you."

Lexi looked up at him, her heart swelling with affection. "And I was drawn to your mystery, your confidence. You seemed untouchable, like someone from a different world."

Beckett stopped walking, turning to face her fully. "But we found each other, despite everything. Despite the secrets, the lies, the fears… we found our way."

Lexi nodded, her eyes shining with unshed tears. "We did. And I'm grateful for every moment, even the hard ones. They brought us here, to this moment."

Beckett leaned in, pressing a tender kiss to her forehead. "I promise you, Lexi, I will do everything in my power to make sure we never go back to that place. You deserve happiness, liberty, and love. And I want to give you all of that."

Lexi's tears fell freely now, but they were tears of joy, of relief. "And I promise to trust you, to believe in us. We've come so far, and I know we can build something beautiful together."

Their walk continued each step a reaffirmation of their commitment to one another. They talked about their hopes and dreams, their fears and insecurities, laying bare their souls in a way they never had before. It was a conversation filled with honesty, vulnerability, and love.

By the time they returned to the penthouse, the sun was high in the sky, casting a bright, hopeful light over the city. They stepped inside, the familiarity of the space grounding them.

"I have something for you," Beckett said, his voice tinged with excitement. He led her to the living room, where a small, elegantly wrapped box sat on the coffee table.

Lexi looked at him curiously, her heart fluttering with anticipation. "What is it?"

Beckett smiled, his eyes twinkling. "Open it and see."

She carefully unwrapped the box, her fingers trembling slightly. Inside, nestled in a bed of velvet, was a delicate silver necklace with a small, intricately designed pendant. It was simple yet beautiful, a symbol of their journey.

"It's beautiful," Lexi whispered, her eyes filling with tears once again.

Beckett took the necklace from the box, gently fastening it around her neck. "It's a reminder," he said softly. "Of everything we've been through and everything we have to look forward to. A symbol of our love, and our independence."

Lexi touched the pendant, feeling the cool metal against her skin. It was a tangible representation of their bond, a promise of the future they would build together.

"Thank you," she said, her voice choked with emotion. "I love it. And I love you."

Beckett pulled her into his arms, holding her close. "I love you too, Lexi. More than anything in this world."

They stood there, wrapped in each other's embrace, the weight of their past lifting with every heartbeat. It was a moment of pure, unfiltered love, a testament to their strength and resilience.

As the day turned to evening, they found themselves back by the windows, watching the city lights come to life. The view was as stunning as ever, but it was the person beside them that made it truly special.

"Do you think we'll ever have a normal life?" Lexi asked, her head resting on Beckett's shoulder.

Beckett smiled, pressing a kiss to her hair. "I don't know what 'normal' means, but I know that as long as we're together, we can handle anything. We'll create our own normal, our version of happiness."

Lexi nodded, feeling a sense of peace settle over her. "I like the sound of that."

They spent the evening talking, laughing, and dreaming about the future. It was a night filled with Inspiration and promise, a stark contrast to the darkness that had once overshadowed their lives. They were free now, free to love and be loved without fear.

Later, as they lay in bed, Beckett's arms wrapped protectively around her, Lexi felt a sense of contentment she had never known before. The road ahead might still have its challenges, but she knew they would face them together.

"Goodnight, Beckett," she whispered, her eyes heavy with sleep.

"Goodnight, my love," he replied, his voice a soothing lullaby.

As she drifted off, Lexi felt a smile tug at her lips. Their journey was far from over, but it was a journey they would walk hand in hand, forever free.

Morning light filtered through the curtains, casting a warm glow over the room. Lexi stirred, feeling the

 gentle rise and fall of Beckett's chest beneath her head. She smiled, savoring the peaceful moment.

"Morning," Beckett murmured, his voice thick with sleep. He tightened his arms around her, pulling her closer.

"Morning," Lexi replied, tilting her head up to meet his gaze. "Did you sleep well?"

"Better than I have in a long time," he said, his eyes crinkling with a smile. "How about you?"

"Me too," Lexi said, her heart swelling with love. "It's amazing what a little peace of mind can do."

Beckett chuckled softly. "Indeed."

They lay there for a while, basking in the comfort of each other's presence. The world outside could wait; this was their time, their moment to savor.

Eventually, they got up, the promise of a new day urging them forward. They moved through their morning routine with a sense of ease and joy, the tension of the past finally dissipating.

"What's on the agenda for today?" Beckett asked as they sat down to breakfast.

Lexi thought for a moment, a playful smile tugging at her lips. "How about we take the day off? No work, no meetings, just us. We could explore the city, do all the things we've talked about but never had the time for."

Beckett's eyes lit up with excitement. "I love that idea. Let's make it a day to remember."

They spent the day wandering through the streets of Manhattan, visiting museums, parks, and cafes. It was a day filled with laughter, shared experiences, and a deepening of their bond. They talked about everything and nothing, reveling in the liberty to be themselves without the weight of their past hanging over them.

As the sun began to set, they found themselves by the river, the city's skyline a breathtaking backdrop. Beckett pulled Lexi close, his eyes reflecting the colors of the sunset.

"This has been the best day," he said softly, his voice filled with emotion. "Thank you for suggesting it."

Lexi smiled, her heart full. "It has been amazing. I feel like we're truly living for the first time." Beckett nodded, his gaze intense. "We are. And I promise you, Lexi, every day will be like this. Full of love, joy, and unrestricted. We've earned it."

They watched the sunset together, the sky ablaze with hues of orange and pink. It was a moment suspended in time, a perfect culmination of everything they had fought for. As the sun dipped below the horizon, the city lights flickered on, one by one, mirroring the stars beginning to emerge in the darkening sky.

Lexi turned to Beckett, her heart swelling with a profound sense of connection. "It's beautiful, isn't it? The way the city transforms from day to night."

Beckett nodded, his eyes never leaving hers. "It is. But it's nothing compared to how you light up my life."

She blushed, a soft smile playing on her lips. "You always know just what to say."

Beckett's gaze was tender as he brushed a strand of hair from her face. "It's easy when you're the most important person in my life."

They stood there, wrapped in each other's embrace, watching the city come alive around them. The intimacy of the moment was palpable, a shared experience that spoke to the depth of their bond.

After a while, Beckett took Lexi's hand and led her to a nearby restaurant with a view of the river. The place was charming and intimate, the kind of spot that felt special and personal. They settled into their table by the window, the soft glow of the candles casting a warm light on their faces.

As they enjoyed their meal, the conversation flowed effortlessly, each topic more profound and heartfelt than the last. They spoke of their dreams, their fears, and the future they wanted to build together.

"You know," Lexi began, her voice thoughtful, "I've been thinking a lot about what comes next for us. We've been through so much, and I'm so grateful for everything we've overcome. But I want to make sure we're heading in the right direction."

Beckett reached across the table, taking her hand in his. "We are, Lexi. I believe that with all my heart. We've faced our past, and we've come out stronger on the other side. Whatever challenges come our way, we'll face them together."

Lexi squeezed his hand, feeling a surge of emotion. "I know we will. And that's what makes me so hopeful. We've built something real and beautiful, and I can't wait to see what the future holds for us."

Beckett smiled, his eyes shining with love and determination. "Neither can I. I'm looking forward to every moment we get to share. You've given me a sense of peace and happiness I never thought I'd have, and I want to spend the rest of my life making you as happy as you've made me."

They spent the rest of the evening savoring each other's company, the world outside fading into the background. It was a night of romance and reflection, a testament to their enduring love.

As they walked back to the penthouse, hand in hand, Lexi felt a profound sense of contentment. The city was alive with possibilities, and she knew that whatever the future held, they would face it together.

Back at the penthouse, they settled into the cozy living room, the soft hum of the city outside a comforting backdrop. Beckett looked at Lexi with a mixture of adoration and anticipation.

"There's something I want to give you," he said, his voice filled with warmth.

Lexi's curiosity was piqued as Beckett reached into his pocket and pulled out a small, velvet-covered box. He opened it to reveal a delicate ring, its simplicity only enhancing its elegance.

"This is for you," Beckett said, his voice steady but filled with emotion. "A symbol of our commitment to each other. I know we've been through a lot, but I want you to know that I'm in this for the long haul. I want to build a future with you, one filled with love, joy, and endless possibilities."

Lexi's eyes welled up with tears as she took the ring from the box, her heart overflowing with love. "It's beautiful, Beckett. Thank you. I can't imagine my life without you."

Beckett gently slipped the ring onto her finger, his touch tender and loving. "It's a promise," he said softly. "A promise to cherish and support you, to stand by your side no matter what."

Lexi looked at the ring, then back at Beckett, her heart full. "I promise the same to you. We've come so far, and I know that together, we can overcome anything."

They embraced, their love evident in the way they held each other. The world outside might have been bustling, but inside their little sanctuary, there was only peace and affection.

As the night wore on, they talked about their plans, their dreams, and the life they wanted to build together. The conversation was filled with hope and excitement, a reflection of their renewed commitment to each other.

Eventually, they made their way to bed, their hearts full and their minds at ease. As they lay there, wrapped in each other's arms, Lexi felt a deep sense of gratitude for the journey they had been on.

"Goodnight, Beckett," she whispered, her voice soft and content.

"Goodnight, my love," Beckett replied, pressing a tender kiss to her forehead.

As she drifted off to sleep, Lexi felt a smile on her lips. The future was bright, filled with endless possibilities and the promise of a love that was strong, true, and free from the shadows of the past.

And so, with the city lights twinkling outside and the warmth of Beckett's embrace surrounding her, Lexi fell asleep, ready to face whatever the future held with a heart full of hope and everlasting love.

EPILOGUE

HAPPILY EVER AFTER

The Manhattan skyline was bathed in the soft, golden hues of the setting sun, casting a warm glow across the city. Beckett's penthouse, perched high above the bustling streets, had become a sanctuary of serenity and love. The once cold, impersonal space now radiated warmth and comfort, a testament to the journey Lexi and Beckett had undertaken together.

Inside the penthouse, the atmosphere was one of tranquility. The expansive windows framed a breathtaking view of the city, their glass panes catching the last rays of sunlight. Lexi and Beckett stood together on the balcony, the soft breeze rustling the curtains and carrying the scent of blooming flowers from the terrace garden. The sky was a canvas of soft pinks and oranges, a perfect backdrop for the moment they were about to share.

Lexi leaned against the railing, her fingers intertwined with Beckett's. She looked out at the city below, her heart swelling with a mixture of gratitude and disbelief.

"It's hard to believe how much has changed," she said, her voice a whisper against the backdrop of the evening.

Beckett's gaze followed hers, taking in the panoramic view of the cityscape. "Sometimes, it feels like a dream," he replied, his voice soft and reflective. "But when I look at you, I know it's real. Everything we've been through has led us to this moment."

Lexi turned to him, her eyes searching his face. There was a depth of emotion there that spoke of both the pain they had endured and the joy they had found. "I never imagined I would find something so perfect," she said, her voice trembling with emotion. "Not just in terms of what we have, but in the way we've grown and changed together."

Beckett reached out, brushing a stray strand of hair from her face. His touch was gentle, almost reverent. "I should have seen it sooner. I was so focused on protecting you from the world that I didn't realize I was pushing you away. I was afraid of losing you, but I see now that I was losing myself in the process."

Lexi's heart ached at his words. She had seen the fear in Beckett's eyes, the uncertainty that had driven him to such lengths. But she had also seen his strength and his love, and it was that love that had guided them through their darkest moments.

"You've changed," she said softly, her voice filled with both admiration and sadness. "We both have. And I wouldn't trade our journey for anything. It's brought us to a place where we can truly be ourselves, together."

Beckett's smile was tender, his eyes filled with a mixture of relief and joy. "That's all I've ever wanted. For us to be able to share our lives honestly and openly. To build something beautiful out of everything we've faced."

The city below continued to buzz with life, a stark contrast to the peacefulness of the penthouse. Lexi and Beckett stood in silence for a moment, simply enjoying the serenity of their surroundings. The penthouse, once a symbol of Beckett's control, now felt like a true home—a haven where their love could flourish.

Dinner that evening was a celebration of their journey and their love. The table was set with care, the flickering candles casting a warm, inviting glow. Lexi and Beckett had chosen a menu that reflected their shared tastes and memories, each dish a reminder of the times they had spent together.

As they sat down to eat, the conversation flowed effortlessly. They talked about their favorite memories, their desires for the future, and the simple pleasures that had come to define their relationship. The evening was filled with laughter and affection, a testament to the bond they had forged.

"This feels like the perfect end to an incredible journey," Lexi said, her eyes twinkling with joy. "And yet, I know it's just the beginning of our new chapter."

Beckett raised his glass, his gaze filled with admiration. "To new beginnings, to love, and to the future, we're building together."

They clinked their glasses, the sound of their toast a harmonious blend of celebration and hope. As they enjoyed their meal, their conversation continued, filled with the easy camaraderie that had always been a hallmark of their relationship.

After dinner, they moved to the living room, where the soft strains of a love song played in the background. The room was adorned with memories of their journey—photographs, mementos, and small tokens that spoke of their shared experiences. The ambiance was intimate and romantic, a reflection of the love that had grown between them.

Lexi and Beckett settled into the plush cushions of the sofa, their bodies close, their hearts even closer. Lexi nestled against Beckett, the comfort of his presence a soothing balm. The quiet of the night enveloped them, the world outside seeming to fade away.

"I've been thinking about what's next for us," Lexi said, her voice soft and contemplative. "About the kind of future we want to build. I know we've talked about it before, but now it feels even more real."

Beckett's hand found hers, his touch gentle and reassuring. "Tell me what's on your mind. I want to hear everything."

Lexi looked up at him, her eyes filled with love and determination. "I want us to continue growing, to keep supporting each other in everything we do. I want us to travel, to explore new places, and to create new memories. But most of all, I want us to never lose sight of what's truly important—to keep our love and connection at the center of everything."

Beckett's eyes shone with emotion as he listened to her. "I couldn't agree more. I want us to build a life filled with joy and adventure, but I also want us to always cherish the little moments we share. It's those moments that make everything else worthwhile."

As they spoke, the city outside continued to shimmer with life. The penthouse, once a symbol of Beckett's control and isolation, now felt like a haven of love and freedom. The walls, adorned with their shared memories, seemed to echo with the laughter and joy they had found together.

The night deepened, and the city below grew quiet. Lexi and Beckett moved to the bedroom, where the soft, intimate glow of the lamps created a soothing atmosphere. The room was a sanctuary of peace, a reflection of the harmony they had achieved in their lives.

As they lay together beneath the soft, luxurious sheets, the quiet of the night was filled with the gentle rhythm of their breaths. Lexi nestled closer to Beckett, her heart at ease. The world outside may have been filled with uncertainties, but within the confines of their love, she felt a profound sense of security and happiness.

"I'm so grateful for everything we have," Lexi murmured, her voice filled with emotion. "For you, for us, and the future we're building together."

Beckett's arms tightened around her, his voice tender and sincere. "I'm grateful for you, Lexi. For your strength, your love, and your unwavering support. You've made my life more beautiful than I could have ever imagined."

They kissed, their lips meeting in a slow, tender embrace. The kiss was a celebration of their love, a promise of the future they would share. As they pulled away, their eyes locked, the depth of their feelings evident in the silent exchange.

The night continued to unfold in a gentle embrace, their hearts full and their spirits at peace. They talked softly about their dreams and plans, their voices a soothing murmur against the backdrop of the city.

As sleep began to take its hold, Lexi and Beckett savored the simple joy of being together. The world outside may have been filled with uncertainties, but within the warmth of their love, they felt a profound sense of fulfillment.

The morning sun would bring with it a new day, full of possibilities and adventures. But for now, in the quiet of the night, Lexi and Beckett embraced their happily ever after. They had faced their past, embraced their present, and looked forward to a future filled with love and promise.

As they drifted off to sleep, wrapped in each other's arms, they knew that their love story was far from over. It was only just beginning, and it would continue to shine brightly, guiding them through every chapter of their lives.

In the end, their journey led them to a place of true happiness. They had faced their challenges, embraced their growth, and found a love that was both enduring and liberating. The future was a canvas waiting to be painted with their dreams, and they were ready to face it together, hand in hand.

With hearts full of love and eyes set on the horizon, Lexi and Beckett embraced their new chapter with assurance and excitement. Their love, forged through trials and triumphs, was a beacon of light, guiding them toward a lifetime of happiness and adventure.

And so, as the night settled around them and the city continued to sparkle below, Lexi and Beckett drifted into a peaceful sleep, knowing that their love story had found its true, everlasting ending.

Printed in the USA
CPSIA information can be obtained
at www.ICGtesting.com
CBHW050604081124
17084CB00033B/1125

9 798218 503390